CHOICES

To Glenn & Helen —
great tennis players!

CHOICES

Mel Goldberg

iUniverse, Inc.
New York Lincoln Shanghai

Choices

iUniverse, Inc.

For information address:
iUniverse, Inc.
2021 Pine Lake Road, Suite 100
Lincoln, NE 68512
www.iuniverse.com

Cover art: an original watercolor by Beverly Kephart

ISBN: 0-595-27527-3

Printed in the United States of America

Youth had seemed to teach that happiness was but the occasional episode in a general drama of pain.

—Thomas Hardy, *The Mayor of Castorbridge*

My thanks to the NAWN (Northern Arizona Writers' Network) for their willingness to let me read this novel as a work in progress.

Thanks to Beverly Kephart, my life-mate, for her artistic talents on the cover, and for her consistent love and patience.

Thanks to Terence Pratt and Mike Cosentino for their early readings and encouragement.

A special thanks to Dan Reid, whose careful reading helped me work out many problems and inconsistencies.

CHAPTER 1

▼

Attorney Robert Morse stopped after work Friday at Murphy's, a bar on Clark near Surf on the near north side of Chicago. Usually, he met friends. Today, he sat alone. He was taking Catherine to dinner, their first date, and he needed a martini.

He had four.

When he got to his Cadillac, he braced his knee against the door to maintain balance as he inserted the key. He started the car, leaned back, and took a deep breath.

"It'll be okay. I don't have far to go, and this'll wear off before I get there." He smiled and patted the steering wheel. The advantage of free legal advice. It was never free.

The dash clock glowed six-thirty. He had promised to meet Catherine at her condo on Commonwealth by seven. A heavy mist had started to roll in from the lake, the kind that might last all night. He turned on the wipers and moved south on Clark Street. Traffic was light.

Catherine had been working as a paralegal for six weeks. It had taken him that long to ask her out because he was forty-two, although he told everyone he was thirty-five. Catherine was twenty-six. Now, he hoped she would invite him to spend the night. He could smell her perfume. He daydreamed about holding her in his arms. When he looked up, the light at Fullerton changed from yellow to red, and he was entering the intersection.

He made the left turn. A woman and a boy appeared in the crosswalk.
Where the hell did they come from?

He hit the brake. The rear of the car skidded on the wet pavement. He automatically corrected.

The woman's arm jerked instinctively toward her son.

There were two distinct thumps. The boy flew over the hood. His shoulder struck the top of the windshield, cracking it, sending instant spider lines, like long thin fingers reaching toward the dash. His body rebounded over the roof and crashed through the windshield of a parked car, his torso supported like a child in a cradle, one arm across his chest, one arm thrown across the hood. The woman bounced away, rolling like a rag doll, arms flailing. She was stopped by a parked car, her shoulder jammed against the tire, her head under it. She was on her back, her legs bent sideways from her shattered knees.

The car skidded to a stop. A rush of adrenaline instantly overcame Morse's lethargy. He pounded his fist on the steering wheel and swore as he waited for the police.

CHAPTER 2

▼

The phone jangled. Sunlight slipped through the mini-blinds putting stripes of light on the bed. Alice Solinsky pulled the worn quilt over her head. She lay on her stomach, wondering how many more months she'd be able to.

Alice heard it ring again. Gregory wouldn't call this early. She expected him to come home in the afternoon.

It rang a third time. She pulled her long tee shirt from under the bed, slipping it over her head as she walked into the kitchen. She picked up the phone on the fourth ring.

"Hello," Alice yawned and ran her fingers through her short hair. "It's seven o'clock in the morning, for crissake." She crossed the room again and sat in one of the two wire-back ice-cream parlor chairs.

"Is Gregory there?" The voice jarred her from early morning drowsiness. It was female. Breathy. Exuding sex.

"No, he's not. Who is this?"

"I was looking for Gregory. Are you one of his roommates?"

"Look Joanie, it's too early for jokes. I only got 5 hours sleep, and I've got an exam to study for."

There was silence on the line, and then the breathy voice continued. "I hoped Gregory'd be there by now. He left here so early, I was still asleep. Will you be sure to tell him I called?"

"Since I'm his only roommate, I'll make sure he gets the message. But you didn't say your name."

"Jean. That's spelled *J, E, A, N.* Just tell him I called." There was a click.

Alice held the phone to her ear until the dial tone hummed. Anger rose in her, like a fire consuming a building. She threw the receiver at the sink that held several glasses and a dish smeared with pizza sauce. The base thumped to the floor. The short cord prevented shattered glass.

Everything in the small kitchen, once simple and romantic, now looked ephemeral and cheap. The cabinets had no doors. She and Gregory had agreed that it was symbolic of everything open, exposed. At least she thought it was.

Alice had moved in with Gregory at the beginning of her junior year at Northern Illinois University. That was a big change in her life. She wanted to go back to warn herself.

"Don't do it. Take Joanie's advice. Don't do it."

Now her life was going to change again. She showered and looked in the long mirror.

She hated her body. Her dark brown hair was too short. Her legs, muscular from playing varsity volleyball, were too heavy. Her hips were too big. Her waist was too thick. She noticed the start of fine blue veins near her right nipple. She knew her appendectomy scar would look horrible when her flat belly became stretched like a balloon. It wouldn't be long before everyone would know.

Her breath caught in her throat. When sound suddenly burst forth, it was a long, wailing sob. "Damn you," she shouted, smashing the side of her fist against the cheap mirror, which cracked under her assault. "How could you do this to me?" The words exploded in her head, echoing like sounds in an empty warehouse.

Just tell him that Jean called.

Alice went back into the bedroom. She dressed and began to clean up. Cleaning eradicated problems. Into a large black plastic bag, she started to throw everything she could find. Old pizza, the pizza box, socks, shoes, Gregory's pants and belt, underwear, anything that was on the floor or on the bed. Then she made the bed and wiped the dresser.

She went to the flat door on cinderblocks at the far end of the living room, almost totally covered with papers and notes, most of which were Gregory's.

"Today's a day you'll remember." she muttered. Using her arm, she swept the desk clear. Books and papers, the pages of his thesis, pens, pencils, everything went flying into the plastic bag, which she dropped over the railing from the deck to the yard below. She looked out the window toward an old maple tree, now filled with spring leaves. The morning sun had just climbed over the house, and the tree sparkled with light and dark green as the wind played shake-leaf in the branches. The black squirrel that she had gathered acorns for last fall was gingerly hunching his way over the street on the thick electrical wires.

But the brightness of the new day could not lighten the pall. At 23, she should have finished college, but she had taken off a year. Her father got her a job at Abbott Labs, where he worked in equipment maintenance. She worked swing shift on the line examining glass bottles for two hours at a stretch. Her co-workers were immigrants who spoke little English or could get no other kind of job. One woman had been a doctor in India, but could not afford an American school to be retrained.

Alice put up with the unwanted comments of the shift supervisor, an Iranian named Ahmadi. He told her she could make more money with her body in one month than a college graduate could make in a year. She always smiled, pretending it was a compliment. One of the Croatian women suggested they cut out his eyes and place them in his chest.

"Ve put dem eye-level vere he alvays look, anyvay."

The year she took off stretched into two.

She should have told Gregory she might be pregnant, but she wanted to be sure. The nurse had called Friday, the day after he left for Chicago to help set up the photo shoot for his father's ad agency.

The dark thought of abortion entered her mind, pushing at her, like someone poking a finger in a softly inflated balloon. Sitting on the sofa, she rocked back and forth silently, closed her eyes, and waited.

CHAPTER 3

▼

It was almost eleven when Gregory Varonian arrived from Chicago. Alice was sitting at the kitchen table.

"I'll make lunch. How was the shoot?" She walked past him to the sink. Iced air buffeted him.

He squinted, wrinkling the dark skin of his cheeks.

"I asked how the shoot went. Do you want to tell me or not." She didn't look at him.

"It, uh, it went well," he stammered. He felt her controlled anger. He had seen her go berserk once in a restaurant, when she had been served bad food. She had thrown the food and the dishes on the floor and stormed out.

"Decent models this time?" she asked. "What hole did they crawl out of?"

"I don't know where my dad gets the models." Gregory chose his words carefully. He set his backpack down by the door, got a beer from the refrigerator, and sat at the table. "Most of them are so skinny that they're almost skeletons. Sorry I didn't call."

"I'm sure you were too busy."

"Yeah, I got pretty involved. With the shooting." He got up and put his hands on her shoulders. He glanced at the desk and changed the subject. "What've you been up to for the past three days? You get the cleaning bug again? Where'd you put my papers this time?"

"I filed them. I need to study more for finals. It's almost the end of the semester. I can't believe we're really going to graduate."

"Are you going to just keep cutting carrots? You've got enough for 10 people."

"Well, someone's got to make salad for dinner, or we won't have one."

"Dinner? What about lunch?"

Alice turned to face him, the knife inches from his face. She waved it as she spoke, and he backed away. "We need to plan a really big blow out. You know, some kind of party where we can say to the world, 'Hey, look at us.' Maybe we can rent the Goodyear advertising blimp, flashing 'College Graduates' in electric lights."

"What the hell's happened?"

"A couple of things," she said in a forced pleasant voice. "I found out Friday that I'm pregnant and you had a phone call from Jean."

Gregory took a step backward and stood with his mouth open, unable to speak. He walked back into the small living room and sat on the sofa. He stared at the floor. The silence lasted for several minutes.

"Well, that's an interesting fucking response," Alice said. "You asked me to tell you what happened, and there it is." She could feel the unwanted tears starting to well up. "Now what do we do?" she asked, her voice breaking.

"Alice, give me a chance to digest the news. It's not what I was expecting."

"Well, getting a call at 7 in the morning from the woman you fucked last night is not what I was expecting either. I thought we had an understanding." Alice wiped her eyes with the sleeve of her tee shirt.

"We did. We do. It's just that something happened." He got up, his arms at his sides and stopped in the doorway. "I can't explain it. It just happened, that's all."

"And what about us. Our plans? Our future? Or is that past tense, too."

"Jean's been working for my dad."

"And one of your responsibilities was to fuck her? I thought we were going to work for him after we graduated."

"Yeah," he mumbled. "But I didn't know he was going to hire Jean. There are lots of other ad agencies. Bigger ones."

"Right. And how many are looking for pregnant graduates?" She picked up a handful of sliced carrots, threw them at him and shouted, "Tell me, you son-of-a-bitch. How many?"

He brushed the carrot slices from his hair and shoulders and stood silently. The knife still in her right hand, she lunged toward him. The paring knife sliced across his raised forearm and fell to the floor. He grabbed her around the waist. She locked her arms around his neck, pushing him backwards into a chair. They toppled over, knocking books and pictures from a small shelf. Gregory's head hit the edge of the table. He lay without moving, blood seeping from the cut on his arm. Alice suddenly felt remorse. At the same time she thought about grabbing the knife from the floor and plunging it into his heart.

"I hope you're dead," she said through tight jaws. She stood and kicked him in the leg.

He groaned, sat up slowly and rubbed the back of his head. It was wet with blood. The smear of blood on his forearm was already scabbing over.

"Are you crazy? You trying to kill me?"

"I wish I had. You're not worth it." Alice walked across the kitchen and picked up the phone.

"What're you doing? Calling the cops? I'm the one bleeding."

Her plans had become iridescent soap bubbles, dissolving as she looked. She dialed the number of her best friend, Joanie, and told her what happened. Then she went into the bedroom and slammed the door.

Gregory went into the bathroom to wash the blood off his arm and try to see how badly the back of his head was cut.

Alice emerged from the bedroom with a cardboard box filled with her clothes. "I'll be back for the rest of my things." There were razors in her voice, but she had regained control.

At Joanie's, she made the appointment at the Planned Parenthood agency on campus. One week later, on a Friday afternoon, Alice packed a few clean clothes in her backpack and Joanie drove her to the clinic.

Three days later, she was lying on a table in the abortion clinic crying, feet in the stirrups, exposed to the cold hands of the doctor she had met at her preliminary appointment.

Joanie held her hand as the doctor explained each step and the purpose of each instrument. The doctor was kind, and spoke softly. If he had shouted, Alice would not have heard him. After the procedure, she lay down in another room. A nurse explained some possible complications and gave Alice a sheet with instructions and phone numbers. When she left, Alice crumpled the sheet and threw it into a corner. Joanie helped Alice out of the clinic. On Monday, they were both back in class.

After graduation, she moved back to her parents' house in North Chicago and starting hunting for a job.

CHAPTER 4

▼

Seven years after Marissa and Andrew Forrest had died, Bill Forrest stepped off the Lakehurst Mall bus at the intersection of Green Bay and Belvedere in Waukegan, sixty miles north of Chicago. He looked at his watch.

At the Amoco station restroom, he looked at his beard, and then walked east. The sweet smell from Dunkin' Donuts made him hungry. He wanted a cup of coffee, but that might destroy his carefully applied disguise. He passed the video store and the between-payday loan company before he came to Eagle Auto Rentals, a shop with only a few older model cars. He suspected they would be more informal with their paperwork than the national chains.

Three years earlier, he acquired a credit card in the name of Edward Forenzi and a post office box in Rockford. On a camping trip to Albuquerque a year ago, he donned his neatly trimmed dark brown beard and acquired a New Mexico driver's license. Six months later, he surrendered his New Mexico driver's license to Illinois. His new Illinois driver's license showed a bearded man named Edward Forenzi. Eddie Forenzi had died in Viet Nam. Bill shook his head in amazement at how easy it was to get legitimate documents in someone else's name.

His beard matched his graying dark brown hair. Although he usually wore jeans, today he had on tan slacks and a pale blue and tan striped sport shirt under a navy blue poplin jacket.

Bill touched the wallet with his new identification. Old business cards gave the wallet bulk. *Now to rent a car, touch nothing, leave unnoticed.* He straightened his shoulders and walked into the store-front agency. The counter was barely three feet from the door and front window. The floor was covered by dirty carpet and the walls boasted several plaques and some antique automobile posters. A door in the partition behind the counter was open, and Bill could see through to a garage where someone was washing a white car.

"Hi. Can I help you?" The man at the counter looked about 70, bald, thin to the point of being emaciated. His thick, round glasses, magnified rheumy, squinting eyes. Bill breathed more easily. This nearly blind old man was probably working to supplement his social security.

"I need a car for a few days while mine's in the shop." He put his hands in his jacket pockets.

"Well, we got a nice one come in this morning. Just cleaning it up now. Four door Chevy Cavalier. $14.99 a day. Couple years old, but it runs good as a new one."

"Sounds fine."

The old man took out a pad of forms, inserted a sheet of carbon paper between the first and second sheet, and wrote down the appropriate information about the car. He handed the pad to Bill to fill out his name and address.

"You paying by cash or credit card, Mr. uh...?

"Forenzi. Credit card. I want a record for my insurance."

That was stupid. Of course I want a record.

"They picking up the tab?"

"What?"

"Insurance. They paying for the rental?"

"Eventually. I have to pay and send them the bill."

"I'll need to see your driver's license, of course."

"No problem. Can't be too careful nowadays."

Bill took out the thick wallet, removing the driver's license and a credit card. The old man stared for a moment at the bearded picture and then at Bill. He held up the license so he could see it with Bill's face.

"Yep, that's you all right." He smiled broadly at his joke. One of his upper front teeth was dark, almost black. Two bottom teeth below it were missing. He looked at the credit card, and put them both on the counter, speaking while filling out the form.

"What do you do, Mr. Forenzi?"

"I'm a doctor. Just joined the staff of Saint Therese, and I got in a little accident."

That was brilliant. Why would they want to rent a car to a man who just had an accident? But the old man didn't even look up.

"Nothing serious?" The old man continued writing.

"Just a little fender bender."

"If you don't want insurance, just initial here." The old man turned the paper toward Bill for his initials, setting the pen next to the form. Bill removed a pen from his own pocket and signed.

He wanted to get the keys and leave, but he didn't want to appear in a hurry. He forced himself to smile. The old man photocopied his license and handed him the carbon copy of the agreement. Bill nodded and folded the paper, putting it in his jacket pocket.

The old man turned and started for the back door. Bill followed him, hands in his pockets again.

"You just wait here. I'll have Alberto bring the car around front."

Bill was glad to walk through the front door and wait on the sidewalk in the small parking lot. As soon as the car was brought to him, he thanked Alberto, and got in, waiting for Alberto to close the door. He put his wrists on the wheel and drove away, stopping at the light to don latex gloves.

Now I have the right weapon.

CHAPTER 5

▼

Alice froze, surprised by the familiar face, slightly distorted in the reflective dark glass of the wall behind the vegetables in the supermarket. She closed her eyes, shook her head slightly, and looked again. There was no mistake. It was Gregory Varonian. She hadn't seen him for six years, since just before graduation. For two years after graduation she killed him in her daydreams. She shot, stabbed and poisoned him. But here he was, pushing a cart and buying groceries at the Jewel Supermarket in Lake Forest.

In keeping with the planned small-town atmosphere of the second wealthiest community in Illinois, the market was small although it was part of an immense national chain. Unlike many others, it offered daily fresh produce and live trout in tanks. Lake Forest still maintained gas lights on tree-lined Green Bay Road.

Alice kept her back to Gregory. She hated shopping on Saturday, but Larry, her husband of four years, worked six days a week, and on the seventh, he drank beer. Alice had weekends off from the ad agency of Harris, Cohan, and Beale. She put two tomatoes into a plastic bag and maneuvered around the young man who was cleaning up a half squashed green pepper.

She moved further away, hoping to escape unseen, inching sideways toward the celery and carrots. She peeked up at the glass. He was still there. Now he was looking at her. She could feel his stare like hot fingers on her neck. She examined the salad dressings, remembering the dip she promised to make for Sarah's party, wondering if Larry would get drunk again and embarrass them.

She held her breath. Gregory was coming slowly, tentatively toward her. The water drops splattered on the glass from the recent spray gave his reflection a grotesque look. His thick black hair was neatly trimmed, and his dark skin made him look as if he had just returned from Hawaii. His mustache had become bushier, a fitting companion to his thick black eyebrows and chilly black eyes. She let her breath out slowly. Her apprehension grew, mixed with the pungent smell of green bananas, making her wince slightly. Her face flushed.

She didn't turn around. She could not believe resentment squeezed her chest after all this time. Her mouth became dry. She stood stone still. Maybe he wouldn't notice her. It worked for rabbits, didn't it? How could he see her? She was a working housewife camouflaged against the vegetables in a supermarket.

"Alice? I'll be damned. I can't believe it. What's it been? Four years? Five years?" He peered around her, close enough for her to feel his breath on her cheek.

Alice put a stalk of celery into a plastic bag. Then she turned around to face him. His voice scraped her like a rasp on flesh.

It's been six years, you shit, "Gregory? What're you doing here?" She swallowed her anger and decided to be civil instead of kicking him in the groin and walking away.

"Buying groceries, same as you."

"I mean here, in town."

"I live here. Now. How've you been?" He smiled as he looked at her. To others, his smile would look sincere, but she knew better.

"I got married. I'm Alice McBride, now." His expression didn't change.

"Oh, yes, that's right." He retrieved his grocery cart, leaning on it as they spoke.

"Larry and I've been married four years next month. You and what's-her-name did get invitations to the wedding." Alice smiled broadly, recalling the fist-clenching joy of addressing that invitation.

"Jean. Her name is Jean."

"Yes, that's right. Jean. She spelled it out for me as I remember? *J, E, A, N.*"

"Congratulations. I know it's a bit late, but I really mean that, Alice."

Alice looked at him sideways, pulling in her chin, "Hey, you're doing well. I read about you in *AdAge.* A full partnership at the agency. You must be proud of yourself." She wanted to add that she had also managed to do well. In spite of him. But why should he care about her small accomplishments.

"You saw that little paragraph? I'm impressed. But Dad always said I'd move up in his agency."

"So it's Varonian *and* Varonian, now. How is old Nishan? Still feisty as ever?" She gripped the handle of the cart tighter as she asked. She disliked Gregory's father, Nishan. She suspected he had probably encouraged Gregory to dump her in favor of Jean.

"He'll never change. He'll stay on at the agency 'till he drops." He straightened his tie. "The agency's his whole life since Mom died. I think it always was. You remember how he is."

Alice resented the reference to his mother as *mom* in a generic sense. It suggested a relationship. She turned her cart and started toward the end of the produce section. She looked at her watch.

"I hear you're with HCB now," Greg continued, following along.

Alice nodded. "About six months now. News gets around. Now I'm impressed." She paused. "So, how are you and Jean doing?" she asked, raising her voice slightly at the name. "She still modeling? Or is that a thing of the past, too?"

"No. I think she's gotten a bit too old for modeling."

Alice looked at her watch again and moved down the next aisle. She really wanted the conversation to stop. She continued to be polite. "But you're a bit over-dressed for grocery shopping, aren't you?"

He spread his arms wide and shrugged. He looked down at his custom-made navy blue suit with a double-breasted jacket, a red pinstriped shirt and a maroon and navy floral print tie. "Doesn't every man dress this way to shop?" He smiled. "Seriously, Jean and I just bought a house, on Waukegan Road. She's meeting some decorator, and asked me to pick up a few things."

"And you came all the way over here? How sweet of you."

"Actually, we just got tired of the Chicago traffic and crime. When we got married last year, we decided to buy a place. Besides, we'd been living together for years. But you know what that's like."

She crushed a box of cereal as she picked it up.

"So, now we all live in Lake Forest. What a small world."

Alice turned her cart and started walking slowly toward the meat counter.

"You mind if I walk along with you?" he asked.

"Isn't that what you're doing?"

He put two thick filet steaks into his cart. "I guess so. I thought about calling you so many times over the years. Just to talk,"

How thoughtful. Why do people say such stupid things?

"Just to talk?" she said. "But you didn't."

"You have no idea how I felt when we split up," Gregory said, now standing alongside her.

Alice put her thumb through the plastic wrapper of a piece of chuck. She turned and looked straight at him, the muscles tightening on the back of her neck. It took a few moments before she was able to speak. "Some things never change," she hissed. "Is that what you were going to call to talk about? How you felt? What about how I felt when you told me about that anorexic bitch." Alice caught her breath. Picking up a lamb chop, she exclaimed, "My God, these things are getting expensive."

"Alice…"

"Don't say anything, you weak bastard. People make decisions for all kinds of reasons. Some we regret, but they can't be unmade. But don't flatter yourself with any guilt."

"It's not like that at all."

"Don't waste your breath, Greg. It doesn't matter now anyhow."

Alice turned the corner and started down the frozen food aisle. "I don't think this conversation is productive. What happened, happened. It's done, over. Now, I really need to get my shopping done."

"I understand. What's your husband doing now?"

"He owns Larry's Garage, over in Lake Bluff."

"On Sheridan near Scranton?"

"Yeah, that's the one."

"Damn. Small world, Alice. I took my car there yesterday for service. I was told he's got a good reputation with foreign cars."

Alice smiled. "He was with Knause for three years."

"Well, you're right. Done is done. Anyway, as you say, we live in the same small town now."

"Don't expect me to say it was nice seeing you again. It was unexpected, I'll say that." She turned to leave, and Gregory touched her arm.

"Wait, Alice." He sounded like a boy pleading with his mother for an ice cream cone. "I'm planning to have a party next month after the decorators are through. Why don't you and Larry come."

Alice imagined the look on Larry's face. *"Oh, by the way, I ran into an old lover at the market. The one I used to live with. I didn't tell you about him because he got me pregnant and I had an abortion. He's invited us to a party at his house.*

"No, Greg. I'm not coming to any damn party at your house." She looked past him.

"Larry doesn't know about us, does he? Well, don't you worry." The condescension in his voice was like molasses. "I'll invite him personally when I pick up my car Monday. That way, no one will be any wiser."

Alice just stared at him as he stood, waiting for her response. "You're joking," she finally blurted out. She walked up to him and stared into his face. "You don't have a fucking clue, do you? I'd sooner walk barefoot over broken glass. Don't be an asshole." She knew there was no way to refuse if he invited Larry. She was caught in a dilemma, and for a moment, wished she had killed him years ago.

He had trapped her again, caught her in the vise of his selfishness and stupidity. Strangers could never crush you like that. Only people you let close to you have that much power. She understood how a man with a gun could kill a friend or family member. She reached into his cart, took out the filets, and ripped opened the package. Holding the Styrofoam back, she jammed the bloody meat into his chest, covering his shirt, tie, and part of his suit with blood.

"God damn you," she grunted, stomping away, leaving her cart filled with food in mid-aisle. She ground her teeth as she stormed off without looking back. Several people stared at him. One of the steaks fell on his shoe, and the other was on the floor between his feet. He was stunned.

"What the hell," was all he could say. "What the hell."

One of the butchers rushed around the counter with a fist full of paper towels, and handed some to Gregory as he wiped at the stain.

"Don't worry about it, it's okay."

The butcher picked up the filets, put them back into the package and tossed them into a trash can next to the counter.

"That woman was crazy mad," the butcher said. "She your wife?"

"No." A smile played at the corners of Gregory's lips. "She just didn't want to come to my party, and that was her way of saying no."

The butcher shook his head. "I'm glad she didn't have a gun. That would've been your blood."

She isn't going to treat me that way and get away with it!

CHAPTER 6

▼

When Larry got home from his garage Monday evening, he stripped off his grease spattered Oshkosh coveralls in the garage.

"Damnedest thing happened today," he yelled as he got a beer from the fridge. "Did some work for a guy on an old Mercedes and he invites us to a party. Just like that. Says he's new in town and wants to get to know the business people."

You mean workers.

"Who was he?" Alice shouted back from the living room. She was glad Larry couldn't see her face.

"Don't know. Said he just bought a place over on Waukegan Road and he likes old cars. He must have a few bucks. Remodeling a big house. Seven bedrooms and seven bathrooms."

"Remember his name?" Alice asked again, knowing the answer, but hoping she was wrong.

"Nah. Gave me his card, though. Needed new plug wires and a rotor. I charged him 400 bucks for the tune-up and he didn't even blink. Just reached in his wallet. Shit. Some people. I'm heading for the shower."

After Alice heard the water running, she walked into the garage. She felt the card in the pocket of his coveralls, and then pulled her hand back. Feeling guilty about looking at the card, she thought she should have Larry get the card himself. As she put the coveralls down, she slipped the card from the pocket. "Gregory Varonian. Partner, Varonian and Varonian," she hissed. She could hear Gregory saying "Nah nah nah nah nah nah," in that nasal sing-song children use to ridicule one another.

"Shit." she threw the uniform toward the wall. It slid along the cement floor.

A choking deep in her throat gripped her. If Larry saw her crying, he'd ask questions. She splashed water on her face and put the newspaper on the table. Larry always liked to read the sports section and have another beer while he waited for her to make dinner.

After a few minutes, he came down stairs, his unruly red hair shiny and wet, with tufts that stood out in different directions. His dark green tank top showed off his muscles and his stylized sunburst tattoo on the back of his right shoulder. Below his beltless tan chinos, his feet were sockless in leather deck shoes.

"Well," He said walking into the garage. "You want to go to some party with rich folks?"

He returned with the card. "Gregory Varonian. Partner, Varonian and Varonian." he read. "Doesn't even say what the hell he does."

"I know the company. It's a small agency. His father owns it." She didn't turn around as she spoke, so Larry was unable to see her face.

"Jeez." He sat in a kitchen chair and unfolded the newspaper. "Sounds like some big money there. That's a party I don't want to miss." He folded the newspaper back to read an article. The rustling grated on Alice's ears. "Gonna be networking," he continued, not looking up from the paper. He pronounced the word slowly, as if it were some prize. "How about that." He brushed imaginary crumbs from the front of his shirt and sat up straight. "I'm going to be networking for big money."

"That all you can think of? Getting money off some rich people?"

"Them bastards been ripping me off all my life. Besides, he's probably got more money than he knows what do to with, and it won't hurt him to throw a little my way. I ain't seen you turning down any paychecks lately."

Alice tried to imagine Larry networking with a group of college educated ad yuppies. They'd laugh at him. Behind his back, of course. None of them would admit that he was more important as an auto mechanic than they were at persuading people to buy things no one needs.

Alice looked out the window. The thought of going to a party at Gregory's new house made the hair stand up on the back of her neck. She stopped peeling carrots and gripped the side of the sink. The knife fell to the floor.

She didn't want to meet Jean. Especially not in Jean's house. They had only spoken once on the phone.

"Hey, what's for dinner?" Larry's question punched into her thoughts. He looked up from the newspaper. "You still alive over there? You been standing at the sink and you ain't moved for a while."

"I just cut myself making the salad. There's a vegetarian lasagna. I'll put it in the microwave. It'll be ready in a few minutes."

"Well, that party could be a real opportunity."

"I don't care for big parties."

"What's the big deal? It's only a housewarming party. You can stay home if you want to, but I want to see how this big money lives. Beside, there's free booze."

You can stay home if you want to. Her father used to say that to her mother whenever they had a disagreement about where he wanted to go. The unspoken end of that statement was *I'll be mad as hell.*

It's only a housewarming party for someone I don't know. Wait a minute. Yes, I think I remember him. He's the one who got me pregnant and then dumped me. And oh yes. Did I neglect to tell you I had the abortion? Must have slipped my mind.

CHAPTER 7

▼

Larry insisted on going in his restored 1965 Mustang convertible. It was a car that caught people's attention. Turning south from Route 176 to Waukegan Road, they came to a small housewarming sign above which floated several black and white balloons. He made a quick right turn, and found himself driving through a wooded area.

"Is this a driveway or a road?" Larry asked, steering the car around several gentle curves. Alice said nothing, watching the trees, wishing she had told Larry about Gregory and her abortion years before. When she and Larry first met, she'd been ashamed to tell him. Now it was too late.

After several minutes of driving, a final curve became a tree lined drive, giving a dramatic view of the mansion. Under a massive overhanging balcony, the drive curved around to the six-car garage and parking area. A uniformed valet opened their doors and gave Larry a number.

"Hey, man, great car."

"Restored her myself." He looked at other arriving guests. He was glad Alice had won the argument about what he should wear.

He wore a navy blue sport jacket with a patterned tie and gray trousers. The jacket could no longer be buttoned across his large chest, which had increased with his weightlifting. Alice wore a cream silk blouse with the top three buttons undone under a western vest and a long denim skirt with western brands as the print motif. Her black western boots were the same ones she'd had since college.

"Women are lucky," Larry had said. "You get to dress like a cowgirl, and I have to wear a jacket and tie. It ain't fair."

Alice smiled.

As they walked up the stairs to the large oak doors, Alice felt her heart beat harder. She felt like a scuba diver in a forest of sea-weed.

The massive oak doors opened. They were directed through the round foyer to a second set of open doors, through which they could see uniformed men and women moving slowly about serving drinks and *hors d'oeuvres*. Alice went to the ladies' room.

Larry looked up at the massive chandelier and admired the silk patterned wall-paper. He walked toward the winding staircase, his feet sinking into the deep green pile of the carpet. He had never been in a house with a winding staircase. He had never even seen one except in old movies. Looking up, he wondered if the second floor would be as impressive as the first. Everyone was busy greeting guests, and without thinking, he walked up the stairs.

Once upstairs, he walked down a hallway with rooms on either side. On the right were rooms that faced the front of the house. He peeked in one and saw it was a bedroom. Walking in and around the large bed, he discovered a walk-in closet and a bathroom. There were French doors leading to a long balcony that ran the length of the house, culminating in the overhang above the front door. The other four rooms on the right were the same. On the left was a double door, locked.

Every bedroom with its own bathroom. If that's the master bedroom and bath, it's as big as the other five bedrooms combined.

At the end of the hallway, he went down the servants' stairway to the kitchen, amid the bustle of people preparing food and carrying trays in and out. They looked at him in surprise, but said nothing. Several women were speaking quietly in a language he didn't understand. He knew it wasn't Spanish.

He returned to the dining room. Walking through the large French doors to the stone patio, he looked over the tents and the yard. Then he went back in to the bar.

When Alice returned from the bathroom, she didn't see Larry. Worried that he would drink too much, she was ready to cry. She took a deep breath. Just as she turned around, she saw Robert Harris coming in. He was the H of Harris, Cohan, and Beale, where she worked.

"Well, hello, Alice," the older man said. At seventy-three, he was the oldest and tallest of the three partners. He walked with a slight stoop, but his brown eyes exhibited the warmth he was known for. "I'm surprised to see you here. Didn't know you were a friend of Greg Varonian."

"Oh, hello, Mr. Harris," said Alice. Her surprise was genuine. She never expected to see anyone at the party who would know her. Telling the truth, she would not have to remember the lie. "Greg and I went to school together."

"Oh? His father and I go way back. You know Nishan?"

"I've met him."

"He's around somewhere, probably talking to a group of young women, the old fool." He laughed heartily. "Well, I've got to find my wife. She hates affairs like this." He walked into the house and Alice started down the stairs toward the parking area.

As she walked down the stairs, she felt like a child in a crowded department store with no hand to hold. She stopped at bottom of the stairs, nodding at some people who were just arriving.

"I hope you're enjoying yourself," said Gregory, coming up from behind her, and putting his hands on her arms. "You fit right in."

Hearing his voice was like diving into an icy pond and gasping for breath. She continued looking out toward the dark woods.

"Greg, don't start any shit." Her hands tightened into fists. "I came to be polite. You know I didn't have much choice."

"Why don't we go out to the bar tent and have a drink." He put his hand on her back and she could feel the pressure, warm on her cool skin. She thought that a long time ago, a different Alice would have turned to face him when he did that, to be encompassed in his arms.

That Alice was a stupid kid.

She started to walk away, her shoes scraping softly on the blacktop, the slight breeze pushing a wisp of hair in her face. She brushed it back with her hand.

"Alice, don't leave. I want to talk." It was a command rather than a request.

She looked back over her shoulder. "About what?"

"About our past. And your future." The breeze suddenly turned cold, and she crossed her arms over her chest.

"I've got nothing to say to you about either."

"Maybe I should talk to Larry. He'd understand. Wouldn't he?"

"What do you mean?"

"You know damn well what I mean."

"You son-of-a-bitch." She walked to where he was standing, her body taut as a guitar string. They walked through the house to the tent in the back yard. She was apprehensive she might see Larry, even though nothing looked suspicious. Larry's jealous nature sometimes got him upset at the smallest things.

She hugged herself as they walked, remaining silent. A few times Gregory stopped to chat briefly. She stopped when he did, frozen as the three foot geisha in the glass box near the fireplace.

At the bar tent, he ordered two glasses of Merlot, and motioned her toward the shadowed space between the tents. They had to avoid tripping over the stretched guy ropes. The smell of ribs and brats mixed with the dank pungent aroma of freshly cut grass. Bits of conversation moved between them. Alice stood with her hand on a guy rope. Gregory stood directly in front of her and put his hand on the same rope, sliding it until it touched hers. She pulled her hand away.

"What the hell is this? What do you want?"

"Look, Alice, I don't know how else to say this. I think about you every day."

"Oh, shit. Is this going where I think it is?"

Gregory continued as if she had said nothing. "Do you remember the first time we made love? After that disaster of a frat party? I've never forgotten it."

"What?" The word escaped from her mouth before she realized she'd said it. The drink slipped from her hand. As the plastic wine goblet hit the ground soundlessly, it came apart, splashing wine on her boots. "You're crazy. This is getting really stupid." She turned to walk away. Gregory grabbed her arm.

"Don't leave your drink on the grass. That's littering." He squeezed her arm and pushed it down toward the goblet. She looked around, fearful. The few people she could see had their backs to them and were engaged in their own animated conversations. She retrieved the goblet and turned to face him, wrenching her arm from his grasp. Her knees quivered.

Alice coughed once, then caught her breath. "Greg, are you crazy? What're you going to do? Drag me to the maid's room and push me onto bed?"

"Just tell me you'd like me to." He put his hand on the side of her neck, and she instinctively pulled away.

"You're out of your mind."

"You could always scream for help. Surely someone here would come to your rescue. Maybe Larry'll hear you. I'm certain he'd find your story interesting."

Her eyes flashed with the fire of hatred, but she said nothing. She felt like a trapped rabbit again, looking for cover.

"Maybe you and I should start again," he said. "With a friendship. I think Larry'd like that. You and I did share a couple of very special years."

She remembered a man she sat with on the banks of the Kishwaukee River, watching a million brilliant pin-dots glitter on the black velvet of a summer night. Now, the stars were overpowered by bright lights. This Gregory had a granite face in harsh light.

"And we still have the future." He pushed gently her toward the front of the tent where guests milled about. She stumbled across the grass. She was safe with so many witnesses. From the house, she heard a band playing a Muzak version of "Rock Around the Clock."

"I'm planning to bring some big accounts in," he continued loudly, as if he were talking to a small group. "Accounts that I might be able use some help with."

"What is this, a job offer? Do you think I'd work for you?"

"You really ought to consider it. Seriously."

The irony of working at Varonian and Varonian ripped through her mind. A group walked by and wished him well in his new home. He smiled, thanked them, and continued to smile as he turned back toward Alice. He looked over her shoulder at another group and waved to them. "You doing anything important at HCB?"

"What the hell difference does it make to you?" Alice saw her chance to walk away. She started across the grass toward the house.

"I don't think you should leave just yet. We still have so much to talk about."

She stopped and looked back at him, standing nonchalantly, the empty goblet in one hand. He motioned her back to him with two fingers.

"I asked what you were working on at HCB?"

"Is this some game, Greg?"

"Of course. You need a refill on your wine. Then, I want an answer to my question. And try to act civilized."

Her voice cracked as she responded. "I'm doing the Cheezie Spread account."

"Oh, yes. Package goods. I do remember package goods. Well, we ought to have dinner some night and talk about it." He looked directly into her eyes. "Just the two of us."

"I don't think so, Greg." She looked around, deciding to call his bluff. "I better get back and find Larry."

The half moon was just rising through the trees, creating a pale orange-yellow glow. She saw Larry coming down the stairs. He stumbled on the last step. She waved to him. He looked at Gregory, cocking his head and wrinkling his brow in an unspoken question. His tie was untied and the two top buttons of his now slightly rumpled shirt were open.

"There you are." His tongue slurred in slow motion. "I been looking all over for you. And with the head honcho himself. Man, this is some place, Mr. Varonian." He spoke loud enough to make others turn. Gregory put his arm around Larry's shoulder.

"Call me Greg. You have an amazing wife, Larry. Did you know that she and I…," he paused and looked at Alice. Her fists balled up like small hammers. Her face contorted with loathing.

Gregory continued, looking directly at Larry. "She and I were talking about the possibility that she might come to work for my firm. What do you think of that?"

"Really?"

"And with a salary increase."

"Damn. That's okay, ain't it Alice. We could sure use the money. People think when you got your own business, everything's great. You know how that is, right?"

"I do know what you're talking about. And I'm glad you appreciate my house, Larry. We'll have to get together some time to talk business and old cars." He squeezed Larry's shoulder, excused himself, and walked away.

"You're so stupid, Larry. Do you really think he gives a shit about you?"

"What do you mean? He's a hell of a nice guy," Larry rubbed the back of his neck.

"Let me have the car keys, Larry."

"Why, don't you think I can drive? I can handle any car made, and you know it."

Alice took the keys from Larry's hand over his faint protests. He fell asleep during the drive home. She wanted to aim the car east and keep driving until they flew over the bluff into Lake Michigan.

CHAPTER 8

▼

Bill wondered if he would be able to do it. Viet Nam was long range. He rarely saw the face of the enemy. He remembered the smoldering remains of a fire-bombed village, and charred lumps he refused to think of as human remains.

He removed his beard, stuffing it into a plastic bag. The bag went into a trash container behind a restaurant. He checked in to Robert's Roost Motel as Richard Newman. Paying cash for the room, he told the clerk that he was from Rockford, and planned to meet friends at Illinois Beach State Park the next day to go on a camping trip in Wisconsin.

After he showered, he lay on his bed, flipping channels on the TV until he came to the news. He stared at the ceiling, listening. *A drive-by shooting at Taylor Street left one dead, two injured. A three year old fell to his death from a tenth floor window at Cabrini Green. A fourteen year old girl was raped by three men in Cicero.*

His fists tightened as determination gripped him. The killing of Robert Morse would be lost in the murder and mayhem that blanketed Chicago's airwaves. Viewers would hardly notice. He and Morse were the only ones who would care. After seven years, it would be good to put his torment to rest.

He closed his eyes, hoping for sleep.

CHAPTER 9

▼

The trial had come a year after the accident. The breathalyzer evidence was ruled as inadmissible because of potentially faulty equipment.

Bill jumped to his feet and shouted. "No! He was drunk. He killed my wife and son!" He was restrained by his attorney. The judge threatened him with contempt.

Morse was fined and given a suspended sentence. The lives of Marissa and Andrew became statistics.

A week later, in the shadow of 14th Street and Interstate 90 near Maxwell Street, Bill bought a .45 caliber Colt. It was a seven-round semi-automatic with a single column magazine. He paid three times the value of the gun, not sure whether to kill Morse or himself. He decided to kill Morse. He would walk up to Morse in broad daylight and blow his brains out. He didn't care if he spent the rest of his life in jail.

As he contemplated prison, he grasped the injustice. Morse's death would be meaningless if he were imprisoned. To be just, the act would have to be planned so only he and Morse would know.

Four years of planning had brought him to Robert's Roost.

As he lay in the dark motel room, he felt the bed move slightly, as if someone had joined him. A hand touched his shoulder. He was afraid to turn his head. Overcoming his fear, he rolled to his left to confront a bloody cadaver alive with worms. Bony arms with skin hanging reached for him.

He sat up, unable to speak, gasping for air, vomit rising in the back of his throat.

"What do you want?" he rasped, his arms across his face in protection.

"Justice. You did this to me and Andrew."

"No, no." He jumped from the bed, gasping for breath, like a man breaking through water to air. He lunged toward the light switch, knocking the water glass and the Gideon Bible to the floor. In the light he saw only pillows on the bed. He sat on the floor, his hand shaking as he reached to pick up the glass.

The next morning, he decided to drive north to Zion, where his would just be another car on the road. After a quick breakfast at Horizzon coffee shop, he drove to Illinois Beach State Park, which was deserted. The old Holiday Inn had been closed for several years, and he knew he could get lost on the hiking trails along the beach near the nuclear plant. Late in the afternoon, he returned to Waukegan and drove to Market Street, parking at the end of the dirt road among the abandoned warehouses and boarded up buildings. There was rubble everywhere and piles of earth higher than his head. He looked out over Lake Michigan and waited. He could make out the Chicago skyline in the distance. He noticed someone move furtively from a gully under the train tracks to one of the deserted buildings, but he knew the homeless derelicts hiding by night in the abandoned buildings would be more interested in their High 10 and Annie Green Springs than in watching him. People here were beyond caring.

At seven o'clock, Bill drove up 8th Street. The evening clouds obscured the sunset.

CHAPTER 10

▼

Robert Morse stood on the steps of the Lake County Courthouse in Waukegan and looked at his watch. Almost six.

A year after the trial in Chicago, he moved to Waukegan to practice law in the firm of Jacobson and Little. He had met Jerry Jacobson in law school, and Jerry had a place for him in his small but growing office.

The weather was chilly, but he wore no coat over his gray Giordini suit. The slight breeze from the lake mussed his thinning hair. He was heading for *The Maroon Room*, a bar across from the bank. Every Friday, he met with a few friends for a drink or two to wind up the week.

As he walked into the bar, he waited a moment for his eyes to adjust to the dim light The room had pretension, decorated in the Victorian style of the 1920s. Ornate, Reubenesque figures lounged over a large mirror behind the bar. Cushioned stools with backs, a brass rail, and a wood bar, coated with polyurethane.

"Hey, Bob." An overweight, balding man turned from the bar as Robert walked in. "How's that probate case coming along?"

"Not bad, George. Probably wind it up next week. Want to be cut in on the estate? Guy left almost two million in property and assets. No trust. Not even a will. All we can do now is file and wait for relatives to come crawling out of the walls. Money seems to bring out the worst in people."

"How old was he?"

"Fifty-two. Couple years older than me. Massive coronary. Doctors are the worst. You'd think they'd take better care of themselves. And their assets."

"If they did, you'd have to go back to chasing ambulances." He laughed at his joke, and all the lawyers at the bar groaned.

"It's strange, you know," Morse continued. "You get up in the morning, do all the things you always do, have breakfast, plan for a little vacation, go through the motions of living, and all the while, you don't know that this day is your last."

"Good thing, too. I don't want to know my last day when I get up in the morning."

Morse thought about the accident that had made him a probate lawyer. He shook his head, dislodging the vision from his conscious mind.

"After that piece of morbid philosophy, Bob, you better buy a round. You may never have another chance." The heavy man laughed as he lumbered from the bar to the table where Morse had joined three others. He signaled to the bartender to bring another round as he sat down.

Two hours later, Robert Morse stood up to leave.

CHAPTER II

▼

The morning after the party, Larry sat at the table in his boxer shorts and a faded green tank top that proclaimed in half-missing letters, "Mechanics Have Longer Hoses." His mouth was dry. His hair stood out from his head, making him look like a circus clown in an orange wig. He looked at the pictures in the sports pages of the Chicago Tribune, but he couldn't focus on the words.

"That coffee ready yet, Babe? My mouth's like a desert."

Alice looked at him and wrinkled her upper lip. "How long you think you can keep going like that."

"Like what?

"Like last night."

"Nothing happened last night. I just had a few beers."

Alice clopped toward him in her leather mules. She wore a blue terry-cloth robe that came to mid thigh. Lips pressed together, she said nothing, and continued to make breakfast. She shook her head, knowing he had given Gregory the opportunity to be condescending.

"I hate that shirt, You know how many people are turned off by it?"

"Nobody I know. How 'bout that coffee?" He rubbed his eyes and yawned. When Alice made no move toward the coffee pot, he got up, looked at the pot, and poured one cup, and carried it the few feet to the table.

"I can't believe you got drunk last night. Great way to get business."

Larry stared at the paper. Alice clattered a bowl on the sink as she beat eggs with a fork. She banged the frying pan on the stove before she put in several strips of bacon. It had been the same way with her mother. Remembering noisy breakfast preparations, she now understood her mother's frustrations. She wanted to scream, to break something, to hit him.

Larry said nothing. As Alice put the plates on the table, she snatched the paper from his hands and threw it on the floor. Larry sat up quickly, looked at her, mouth open, eyes wide.

"You are a piece of work." She slid a plate of scrambled eggs and bacon in front of Larry and crumpled in her chair.

"What the hell do you want me to say. I'm sorry. That better?"

This was one of the times when she wanted to walk out the door keep going. Get a plane to her sister's in California. It would be so easy. But she heard her mother's voice in her head.

People are supposed to stick with it, no matter what. That's what life is all about. Making choices and sticking with them, even when they turn out to be foolish or painful.

It amazed her that Larry was so blind. He put a forkful of eggs into his mouth, swallowed, and started talking.

"Y'know, that Varonian guy, he's not so bad. Knows a lot of people. And looks like he's got more money than he can spend in one lifetime."

"He thinks you're a drunk. Don't you know that."

"All I had was beer. And you can't be a drunk if all you drink is beer. Everyone knows that. Drunks need whiskey. Like my old man. So lighten up, will ya? And how the hell do you know what he thinks. You sound like you know him, for crissakes.

"I do know people like him. People who think if you're a mechanic, you're not worth shit."

"Yeah. Well you don't know as much as you think, college girl. I'll tell you what I know. It'd be good to have him as a friend."

"A friend? Why the hell would he want you as a friend?"

She scraped her eggs into the sink, and poured herself a bowl of corn flakes with skim milk.

A friend is someone you have things in common with. Someone you can share your innermost secrets with. Someone who will tell you honestly when you screw up, and will stick with you to help you make things right again.

"I'm your friend, Larry, but you don't even realize it."

"Yeah I do, Babe. But you don't know nothing about this. It's politics. That's what business is nowadays, politics. He said we ought to get together sometime. Or don't you remember."

"I don't think he really meant it. It was just something to say."

They finished their breakfast in silence.

Larry couldn't understand why Alice had such a negative attitude about Gregory. Larry wanted Varonian's business, and hoped to attract other wealthy people who wanted to keep their Ferraris and Porches running well. He looked at the back of her head. *A college education, but she sure didn't understand the business world.*

Alice didn't want to let Larry make a fool of himself, but she couldn't tell him the truth. She picked up the pan that had scrambled eggs a few minutes before and moved it to the sink. Then she put it back on the stove, as if she had forgotten something and wondered what to do next.

Larry picked up the paper from the floor, and sipped his coffee. He pushed his chair against the wall and leaned back, watching the toaster silently. When the toast popped up, he placed the slices on a plate and smeared jelly on them with a spoon. Then he sucked the jelly off the spoon and his fingers and wiped them on the shirt, which was already badly stained.

"What the hell's wrong this morning. You got any idea what the potential is here?"

"Apparently not."

"Aw, shit. I don't want another fight. I got too much work today."

"Gregory Varonian's on another planet. We've got nothing in common with people like him."

"I know what the problem is. You don't think I'm smart enough." He swallowed. "You think he's better'n me 'cause he's got money and a college education. Right?"

"That's not what I meant and you know it, dammit."

"Just 'cause you work with all them white shirts don't mean you know shit about people like him."

Alice could never win this argument. Larry, like many people, believed the more money a person made, the more successful he was.

"I gotta go to work. He grabbed his work shirt from the back of the kitchen chair and walked toward the front door. "Be home around six," he shouted over his shoulder as he walked through the door.

Alice sat at the table and cried until the helpless feeling passed. She would have to go along with Larry's plans. Once again, she wished Gregory dead. That would solve all her problems.

CHAPTER 12

▼

The following Sunday afternoon, Larry sat in his overstuffed chair watching TV, feet up, beer in his hand, and chips in a bowl on his lap. He heard Alice cleaning up after dinner. He didn't get up.

The shelves on the wall above the TV held encyclopedias and an array of decorator-type books propped up to show their covers: *Chicago from the Air, Great Buildings of Moscow, Historic Places of America*. There were also many hard-back and paper-back books which had been Alice's. Adding them to the decor was her attempt to give the house an ambiance of education and learning. As Larry watched highlights from the Bulls game, Michael Jordan floated through the air in slow motion and slammed the ball into the hoop.

Alice walked in from the kitchen after cleaning up from dinner. "I'm going upstairs. I need to read over some material for my meeting tomorrow."

"Looks like the Bulls'll make the playoffs. Damn, what I'd give to get tickets. I hear they're going for 500 bucks apiece."

Alice started up the stairs, shaking her head. *Why would people spend a week's salary to watch millionaires play a game which had no real-life value. People are still homeless, children are still hungry, and poor pregnant women have trouble getting abortions.* That thought always lurked in the back of her mind.

As she was half-way up the stairs, Larry shouted, without taking his eyes from the TV. "Hey. Guess what. Talked to Gregory Varonian today. He came by the shop. Told me about his cabin. Up in Fish Creek. His old man it bought years ago."

Alice gripped the handrail. She sat on the carpeted steps and turned her face toward the wall, glad Larry was glued to the TV. "Where's Fish Creek?" A scene of her and Gregory jolted through her mind, limned in a flash of lightning. They sat on an old wooden porch swing watching the sun set on a warm, humid summer evening. Their bathing suits were still damp from an evening swim. Gregory lay on his back, his head in her lap as she stroked his head and played with the thick hair on his chest.

"It's about five hours north of here, he says. Up in Door County. Wisconsin. Greg says the fishing's great up there. And he just bought a boat. Docked at Egg Harbor, wherever that is. And he said—you ready for this—it'd be nice if we'd come up there sometime."

"That's nice," she said. After a few moments she got up and continued up to the bedroom. She couldn't concentrate. Gregory was turning her life upside down again.

Why can't he just leave me alone? Why can't he just die and leave me alone?

Gregory called the next evening. Alice froze when she recognized his voice. Then she spoke quietly, not wanting Larry to hear.

"Greg, why're you doing this to me? What do you want from me?"

Blood was thrumming through her head, and for a moment, she couldn't focus her eyes.

"Not even going to ask how I got the blood out of my shirt?"

"I don't care."

"I threw the shirt and tie away. But the suit was another story. The cleaners said…"

"Stop it. What do you want?"

"We're going up to the cabin next weekend," he said. "Haven't been up there for while because of work. How about you and Larry joining us?" Alice could hear the smirk in his tone. "I'd really like it, Alice."

"You know what I'd like," she stage-whispered.

"No. Tell me."

Before she could respond, Larry walked into the room. Alice relaxed her voice into a normal conversational tone, while every fiber of her body was screaming *No! No! No!* Her fingers held the phone in a death grip wishing it were Gregory's throat. "I don't think we can make it. Maybe another time."

"Is that Greg? He said he'd call this evening." said Larry, walking over to her and pulling the phone from her hand. "Hey, Greg? What's happening?" Then, with his hand over the mouthpiece, he grunted, "What the hell do you mean 'another time'!"

"Damn right, we can. You know women. No spirit of adventure."

Alice turned and walked slowly toward the stairs. She felt like a dog who was harshly reminded he could only run to the end of his chain.

CHAPTER 13

▼

Bill looked at his watch in the glow of the halogen street lamp. Five minutes to eight. For forty-five minutes, he had been parked just east of the overpass, under the Public Library sign. He started the engine, pulled forward into the yellow zone, and looked toward the police station on his left. Traffic was light. People were either at home eating dinner or in the bars celebrating the end of the week.

Adrenaline pumped through his veins. His heart punched his chest. He was back in Nam, waiting for the command. But now he gripped the steering wheel instead of his M 16.

Then Morse appeared. He walked from the bar to cross Washington in the middle of the block.

Bill moved across the intersection. Morse looked directly toward him, but could not see inside the dark car. Morse stepped off the curb. Bill slowed, as though to let him cross, keeping one foot on the brake and the other on the accelerator.

One car passed Bill's on the left, forcing Morse to wait. He was now directly in front of Bill's car. Bill jammed his foot down on the accelerator. The car jumped forward. Morse saw the Chevy hurtling toward him, less than twenty feet away. He could have dived for safety, but he froze with shock.

He believed there are consequences for every action, whether or not we know them. His shoulders slumped like a man facing necessity in a fatalistic universe.

The bumper of the Cavalier caught him just below the knees, cracking his legs. His upper body was snapped down against the hood with such violence that his shoes flew off. The side of his face slammed against the hood and slid up to the windshield. The impact tightened Bill's body against the seat belt, as the car flew across Genesee Street. The flesh of Morse's cheek scraped off when it slid across the hood. His bloody cheekbone and ear pressed against the windshield as if he were listening for a heartbeat. His right eye bulged from the socket, impaled by the windshield wiper. His mouth, open in a grotesque smile, showed broken teeth imbedded in ripped lips.

Bill slowed to dislodge the body, but it clung with ferocity. He jammed the accelerator to the floor. The car lurched across Sheridan. Entering the seldom used Amstutz Expressway, he pulled the wheel hard to the right. Morse's body flew from the hood, arms over his head like someone waving good-bye. His body smacked against the low concrete wall of the on ramp, his legs extending into the traffic lane.

Bill accelerated down the ramp, moving south. As he approached Belvedere, he slowed, maneuvered the car across the grassy median, and headed north. The expressway ended at Greenwood, less than two miles ahead. When he passed Washington Street, he heard sirens. On the verge of panic, he slowed again, recrossed the median, and stopped the car on the dirt shoulder. He lurched out, happy for the darkness. He stumbled across the railroad tracks before he stopped to catch his breath in the trees and bushes. Climbing the embankment toward the houses on the east side of Sheridan Road, he was stopped at the top by a chain link fence. A dog barked. He scrambled along the fence for fifty yards before he came to an unfenced yard. Once on the street again, he brushed himself off, put his latex gloves in his jacket pocket, and walked back toward the Washington Street train station. He saw the pulsating flashes of red light from the police cars, one of which was blocking the entrance to the expressway.

He had not planned to kill Morse. Death was too easy. He wanted Morse to live a long time in pain, as he would live the rest of his life with emptiness. But he was not angry. What was done was done, and could not be undone. After seven years, he could now get on with his life.

CHAPTER 14

▼

Larry and Alice arrived at the Varonian estate a little before nine. They parked their car next to the six-car garage. One of Gregory's live-in house staff put their bags in Gregory's Cadillac. Jean informed them that Gregory was on the phone, but he would be right out. Larry looked at the Cadillac. Jean and Alice smiled at each other in an awkward silence.

"How's the new house?" asked Larry, when Gregory walked toward them.

"It's everything I always wanted. Spacious rooms, a large entertaining area, and as many bathrooms as there are bedrooms," Jean laughed. "We can have house guests and never see them until dinner. I love it."

The once skeletal model wore Levis and a blousy tee shirt with a hand painted woodsy scene. Her make-up gave her a deep-eyed look. She showed no indication that she knew about Gregory's past involvement with Alice.

The Alice and Gregory Story. Pregnant Alice abandoned, forced into abortion. Maybe I ought to thank her.

The coolness of the leather felt good on Alice's skin. She folded her arms, leaned against Larry, and decided to make the best of this horrible situation. For Larry and for her marriage, she would swallow her anger and suffer Gregory's smirking for the next three days. Alice had no idea how difficult the weekend was going to be.

Gregory turned north on Waukegan Road and then west on Rockland Road. As they passed the residential facility for mentally challenged adults known as Lamb's Farm, Gregory asked Larry if he had ever eaten at the restaurant.

"Nah, the place gives me the creeps. I got nothing against them people. They can't help what they are, but I ain't gonna eat there."

"Well, the food's good. I think it's a wonderful place for those handicapped people who can't make it in the outside world."

"So, Alice," said Jean, as Gregory turned north on the Tri-State Tollway toward Milwaukee, "I was a bit surprised when Greg told me that you and he knew each other in college."

Alice saw Gregory's face in the rear view mirror. His forehead was drawn into furrows. The back of Alice's neck became taut, the hairs prickling.

"Yes," he said, not waiting for Alice respond. "After you told me you went to Northern, I checked my old yearbooks, and there you were. I think we might have had a class together. We both had similar majors."

Alice sat back, relaxed. "I think I'd remember if we had a class together. It wasn't that big a school then."

Larry looked at Alice. "You two knew each other?"

"It was a long time ago," said Gregory, "and we really didn't. I was too busy partying back then." he spoke to the steering wheel.

Larry folded his arms and leaned back. He looked straight ahead.

As the car passed Abbott Labs, Jean said, "Gregory also tells me that you work for Harris, Cohan, and Beale. Any special project?" She didn't turn around as she spoke, and Alice had to lean forward to hear.

"Actually, I work for Results. It's a subsidiary of HCB. Packaged goods. I'm on the Cheesie Spread account."

"Didn't you go after that account last year, Greg?"

"I thought about it, but we don't have any decent package goods people."

They passed the Great America Theme Park. "Now there's my kinda place," Larry said, pointing to the giant structure which loomed 80 feet above them. "Shows and roller coasters."

"Sounds like you may be ready for a new job, Alice." Jean ignored Larry's comment. "You ought to think about coming to work for us. With your background, I'm sure Gregory would find a place for you." She paused and looked at Gregory. "Wouldn't you?" Her last comment sounded more like a command than a question.

"Always have a place for good people," he muttered.

"Thanks. You never know when the ax is going to fall in this business." Alice looked at the rear view mirror again, but Gregory was staring at the road ahead.

Alice glanced at Larry, who still sat with his arms folded, showing he was upset.

Conversation stopped, and quiet settled like a black wool blanket, broken only by the low hum of the highway and the whine of the occasional truck that they passed at 80 miles per hour. When they passed Mars Cheese Castle, Alice remembered she and Gregory had often stopped there for fresh cheese curds. He'd always called the curds squeaky cheese.

As they approached Milwaukee, Gregory broke the clumsy hush. "Hey. Why don't we stop for lunch at Smith's Fish Shanty in Port Washington."

Everyone muttered in assent. Here was something they could agree on.

"It's one of my favorites. I used to stop there a lot when my dad and I came up here."

Don't I remember. We always made the Fish Shanty stop too. Why don't you mention that, too?

"That's an odd name for a restaurant," Alice commented. Gregory's cheeks rose slightly in a smile. They'd referred to it by other names, like 'Our Secret Hideout.'

They had sat at an outdoor table drinking beer in the summer, and close to the fire in winter, drinking hot chocolate with peppermint schnapps. They were here again, now married to different people and pretending they barely knew each other.

In the restaurant, Larry continued to be mute until Gregory mentioned fishing. Then Larry opened up. He told Gregory about the one time he had gone deep sea fishing off the coast of Florida with some buddies on leave. Alice had heard the story so many times she hated it, but she smiled politely and listened as if it had been the first time. Then Alice told about the times she had gone fishing with her friends in North Chicago.

"I had one friend, Marianne Tortorola, whose father loved to fish. He was from Italy. He'd take a bunch of us kids out to the lake on weekends. Mostly we went up by the Nuclear plant in Zion. We joked that the fish were bigger there, and their eyes glowed in the dark.

"What about your father?" asked Jean.

Alice paused. "My father was too busy. He worked most weekends. Marianne's father had his own business. He was a tailor, and had a small shop in Wilmette. But he did have one rule," she laughed. "It was aimed at us girls." Alice imitated a man's Italian accent. "You gotta hook-a you worm if-a you wanna hook-a you fish."

Everyone laughed.

Larry shook his head slowly and looked at her. He spoke quietly, shielding his voice from the others. "I guess there's lotsa things I don't know about you, huh?"

CHAPTER 15

▼

Looking at the menu, Alice decided to be contumacious. She asked Jean how she and Gregory met. Larry had finished a beer and ordered another.

"I'm afraid it's not much of a story," said Jean. "I was doing a promo for Borden's milk, I think. Or it could have been Dean's. Y'know, I don't really remember. But I know it was just before Gregory graduated from Northern. We realized we had a lot in common."

I bet you did. Alice nodded. She smiled at Gregory, who appeared to study the menu, his skin purpling. Alice suspected Jean had no conscious part in the break-up years earlier.

"What do you recommend, Gregory?" she said, speaking to the open menu across from her. "You've been here before. What's good?"

"I think I'm gonna have the fish plank with French Fries," said Larry, not waiting for Gregory to answer. Beer and the thought of food helped his mood. He smiled at Jean. Jean was polite, and smiled at Alice.

"Good choice," responded Gregory. "So will I."

The food came. Alice and Jean ate in silence. Alice looked around at the thick hawsers forming a passage-way, and the square bar in the center of the dining room. Through the window she saw the lake was dotted with sail boats. Brilliant blues, reds, greens, and whites, like a Renoir painting.

Larry downed his fourth beer and asked Gregory how he liked the Cadillac.

"I'll like the new one better," Gregory said, picking up the check.

"It's one of the best built American luxury cars, and costs less than a Lexus."

Gregory looked at his watch. "Sorry to bring this to an end, but we still have a couple of hours to go."

As if everyone has been waiting for his decision, they all pushed their chairs back and grunted in agreement.

Gregory followed route 42 north through Manitowoc and Two Rivers. They watched the waves crash along the shore of Lake Michigan. Half an hour after crossing the bridge in Sturgeon Bay, they were at the cabin in Fish Creek.

It was a two-bedroom wood frame house. The one bathroom was in the hall that led from the kitchen to the bedrooms.

Jean suggested they all go fishing at daybreak. "I always heard the best time for fishing was early in the morning. And I've always been a morning person."

"Sounds good to me," said Larry. He looked at Gregory.

"I'm beat from the drive," said Gregory. "I'll pass this time. I'm sleeping in."

"You two go ahead," said Alice. "This is one fishing trip I hope I don't catch a thing." She saw the surprised look on Larry's face. "I just want to relax," she continued.

"But I thought you liked fishing," said Larry following her into the bedroom.

"I do, but I just want to relax and vege out in the morning. I've had a horrible week at work, and I had to fight just to get the day off."

Larry closed the door. "What the hell's going on here? First I find out you knew Gregory before, but you didn't tell me. Then I find out you went fishing regularly as a kid and loved it, but you don't want to go tomorrow with me. You figure to get it on with him?"

"Don't be stupid. I really didn't know him." I only thought I did.

She thought about Diane, a friend whose husband left her.

"I know my husband like a book," Diane had told Alice. "He's so predictable."

A month later, Diane's husband told her he didn't want to be married any longer, and walked out.

What person really knows the mind of another? We delude ourselves to think we know other people.

"It just seems weird, that's all," Larry said as he walked out of the bedroom. "Really weird."

Alice sat on the edge of the bed, and Larry went into the living room to watch TV. She was glad the bedroom door locked. The next day, she would be alone in the house with Gregory.

When Larry came to bed that evening, Alice asked him if he were still upset.

"Hell, no." he replied. His blue eyes twinkled in the soft light of the small table lamp. "Jean and I'll have some fun."

"Yeah, I saw how you stared at her during lunch."

"Well, at least I didn't know her for years and not tell you." He undressed and got into bed. Lying on his side with his back to Alice, he hugged himself with his arms, and went to sleep.

For a while, Alice lay staring at the ceiling. The light of the half moon was bright enough for her to make out dim shapes in the room—the chair draped with clothes, the dresser with the lace cover, the decorative wash bowl and water pitcher, and the photo of two adults and a child in the silver frame. She couldn't make out the faces, but she knew who they were: Gregory's parents and Gregory. After what seemed like an hour, she rolled over on her stomach and fell asleep.

The sound of Larry opening the drawer and putting on his bathing suit woke her. Two slivers of orange light eased in. Larry raised the shade, and the rosy glow of the eastern sky spilled through the window, giving a peach luster to everything in the room. With sleepy eyes, she peered through a slightly opened door and watched Larry and Jean head out the door with their gear. Larry wore a light-weight Gold's Gym sweat shirt with the sleeves torn off, showing his well-muscled arms and shoulders, and dark green boxer swim trunks. Jean wore one of Greg's black and white pullover nylon jackets that hung to her thighs like a micro-mini skirt. No doubt she wore a bikini swimsuit underneath. Either that or she wore nothing under the jacket. Alice wanted to wish them luck, but they were gone before she could say anything.

About an hour after they had gone, she slipped on her cotton robe and walked down the hall to the bathroom. When she opened the door to come out, Gregory was standing in the hall, wearing a dark blue terry cloth robe.

"Alice, this is insane. Dammit, you remember when we were here. We made love on the floor, on that rug."

He took a step closer. Alice pulled her robe closer around her and backed up. Gregory grabbed her arm and pulled her toward him, sliding his other arm under her robe next to her skin. Instinctively, Alice put her arms in front of her, fists balled up under her chin. An angry childlike feeling radiated over her. She pushed him, but his grip was strong.

"Are you crazy? If Larry finds out, he'll kill you."

Gregory pulled her tighter, forcing the side of her head against his chest, her breasts now pressed against his skin.

"But he's not going to know, is he?" He repeated louder, into her ear, "Is he?" Gregory paused. "Because you don't want him to know about us, and about our little secret, do you?"

Gregory put his hand under her chin and forced her head up to kiss her. Alice swung her arm to slap him. As her arm slashed through the air, Gregory caught her wrist and held it. Grabbing her other wrist, he pushed her down, forcing her to her knees on the floor.

"That's a good position. Now, you be a good girl, and no one will know anything." She turned her head to the side and started crying.

"You son-of-a-bitch," she grunted through clenched teeth. "You rotten son-of-a-bitch." She wrenched one arm free and flailed wildly, striking him on the leg. He let go her other wrist and she fell to the floor. She ended on her back, her robe flying open. She rolled to her stomach and pounded the floor with her fist. Her nose was pressed to the wood floor. Tears puddled under her eyes.

"Are you crazy? I have no intention of doing anything here, now. I just want you to know how things are." He went into the bathroom and closed the door.

Alice slowly rose, pulled her robe tightly around her, and ran back to the bedroom. She sat on the edge of the bed. Her head pounded, and her legs shook. She reached inside for strength she hoped was there.

A thought nagged at her. The best thing would be to tell Larry and get this out in the open. Would Larry want to hear that his new, rich friend once got her pregnant? *I'm the one who didn't want to go fishing, and chose to stay at the cabin with Gregory. I'm the one who didn't tell Larry that Gregory and I once lived together.*

She decided to say nothing, to hope this was a one-time thing. She just wouldn't be alone with Gregory for the remainder of the weekend.

"This is insane," she said out loud, locking the door. She alternately cried tears of rage and self pity. She climbed back into bed, not taking off her robe, and pulled the sheet up to her chin. Staring at the ceiling, she tried to make sense out of what had happened. After a while, she fell asleep.

It was almost noon when Jean and Larry burst in. The noise woke Alice. Larry emptied brown trout and pan fish into the sink.

"Your wife's some kind of fisherman, Greg. Most of these are hers. She had two trout almost before I could bait my hook."

Gregory looked at the fish.

"I guess it's fish for dinner tonight," he said. "Anybody want any lunch? I'll make some sandwiches while you two clean up."

Alice opened her door and stepped out, dressed in gray sweats.

"We caught 'em, so you and Greg have to clean and cook 'em," laughed Jean.

"I think you and I ought to cook them, Jean," said Alice. If Gregory cooks like Larry, we'll have either burned or raw fish. Gregory can clean them."

"No problem," said Gregory. He put the fish in plastic bags and set them in the refrigerator. Alice poured herself a cup of coffee, and sat down. She feared the future. Larry would remember the job that Gregory had now offered twice. Staring into her coffee, she closed her eyes and sighed, wishing for the weekend to end.

CHAPTER 16

▼

Monday, Alice had coffee and a Danish at the Scranton Cafe in the train station before catching a late train. She had nothing on her calendar until her lunch meeting with the Cheesie Spread people.

Larry was in his mute mode, speaking only in grunts. She needed to get a handle on whether to tell him and get everything out in the open.

If I tell him, he'll blow up and accuse me of lying. It might be the end. He'd never trust me again. And how can I trust him, now that he's been betrayed?

On the other hand, if I don't tell him, I'll be in Gregory's power, and judging by the weekend, that won't be pleasant. How the hell did my life turn into this mess?

She walked to the platform and then had to run back for her briefcase. Unlike the white-shirt special, as Larry called the early morning commuter, this run was filled with an assortment of shoppers and students, as well as many business people. She found a seat on the aisle and took a folder out of her briefcase. Across the aisle, a shred of a conversation drifted her way. Two young women, who appeared to be college students, were having a whispered discussion, heads bent near each other.

"You got to tell him."

"How can I? He'd kill him. Or he'd kill me."

"He ain't that crazy. You just can't play him any more."

The two women leaned closer to each other. Alice was unable to hear any more, but hugged the folder and shut her eyes.

What a phrase. Play him. Like landing a fish. Am I playing Larry or is Gregory playing me?

She opened the folder and tried to read her notes for the meeting, but couldn't keep her mind from replaying the past weekend.

Why is Gregory doing this to me? He has everything.

She closed her eyes again tried to imagine a scene where she told Larry everything The train jolted, iron wheels screeched on iron tracks. Alice was jerked back to reality.

She crossed her legs and stared at the minute imperfection, a small knot, just above the knee of her white stockings. She reached to pick at it and stopped, knowing she would make a hole.

That's life. A knot appears, and you wonder if you should pick at it or leave it alone. She decided there was nothing she could do.

Besides, Larry won't believe me. He'll think what happened over the weekend was all my fault.

CHAPTER 17

▼

It was almost four in the afternoon when Bill Forrest finished with his last conference for the day at Roosevelt High School. He walked toward the English Office, a small room and with one window and four desks crammed between shoulder-height filing cabinets. The work space in the center of the room consisted of a folding table which was littered with papers and books.

As Bill opened the door, two men were speaking quietly with Melanie Knight, the department chairperson. As soon as he entered, they abruptly stopped. She walked toward him, giving him a furrowed-brow look that could not be seen by the others.

"Bill, these, uh, men want to talk to you. They're detectives."

"Thanks, Mel. Is this about that suspected child abuse case?"

She shook her head slowly side to side. Bill faced the two men as they showed their badges.

"I'm Bill Forrest." He put his briefcase down so he could shake hands, but the detectives remained motionless.

"I'm Don Walker and this is Jeff Spritzer. We need to ask you some questions. Is there some place we can talk?"

"Sure. We can talk in my room. It's empty now." Then he turned as he reached the doorway. "See you tomorrow, Mel."

Once in the hall, Walker began talking. "We're from homicide. We need to talk to you about a hit and run accident." Walker was about 50, wore a blue gabardine suit, shiny at the elbows and knees. He was slender, with a salt and pepper crew cut, a few inches taller than Bill. Spritzer, in his early 30s, balding and stocky, wore a gray, double breasted suit with a slightly wrinkled navy and tan striped tie.

At the end of the hall, Spritzer spoke. His voice was nasal, as if he had chronic asthma.

"Can we can get a cup of coffee somewhere?"

"Sure," Bill responded. "At the end of the block there's a Burger King. Over on Kimball and Leland. We call it the student lounge. The place should be nearly empty by now."

The three men walked along Kimball, three abreast. No one spoke for a few minutes.

"Robert Morse got killed night before last," said Walker, just before they entered the Burger King…

"Yeah. Hit and run. Right outside the courthouse in Waukegan," added Spritzer. "Know anything about it?"

"Wow," said Bill. He paused for several seconds, his hand on the door. He had rehearsed his response. Surprised but glad. "I can't say I'm sorry. I'm sure you know the story or you wouldn't be here."

If they could link me to the killing. I'd be arrested by now.

"We just wondered if you knew anything about it," asked Walker.

"Not really." He felt he had been holding his breath and he was able to let it out. "I don't think I've even been in Waukegan since the trial. That's been at least four years."

"His trial really pissed you off, didn't it." said Walker.

"Damn right it did. But there wasn't anything I could do about it. The city attorney told me that suing him for wrongful deaths could drag on for a long time. I didn't want to go through it all again. Besides, what good would some money do me?"

"Interesting attitude. So what'd you do?" asked Spritzer.

"Nothing. I just wanted to get the whole thing behind me."

"You didn't happen to rent a car recently, did you?" asked Walker.

"No. Why?"

"Morse was hit by a car rented to…" Spritzer paused as he pulled out a small notebook. "To one Edward Forenzi. Ever hear of him?"

"No. No, I don't think so."

"We did a little checking. He was killed in Viet Nam. He was in your unit."

"That so? Well, there were a lot of guys in my unit. Their faces changed every week. Didn't really get close to anyone. Didn't want to."

"Yeah. I know what you mean. I was lucky. Got hit in the leg with mine frag-
ments and went home."

Forenzi was lucky, too. He died quick.

"So where were you night before last? That is, if you weren't in Waukegan."

"I was home, grading papers. Alone. Teaching English means a lot of paper
grading."

"Alone."

"Yes, alone. I don't like distractions when I grade papers. Y'know, people who
live alone are usually alone. If I had known Morse was going to get himself killed,
I'd have arranged for someone to watch me.

The two men got up. "Thanks for chatting with us, Mr. Forrest. We'll be in
touch," said Walker. "We might need you to come in for a line-up. By the way,
when did you shave your beard?"

This guy's been watching too much Columbo.

"Beard? Never had one. Tried to grow one in college, but it was too scraggly."

They turned and left. Bill sat there finishing his coffee, wondering if the man
with the thick glasses could identify him. He was glad the detectives had come to
see him. He hoped he convinced them he had been unaware of Morse's death.
He drained his styrofoam cup and stood. His legs now felt strong enough to support his weight.

CHAPTER 18

▼

Alice's heels clacked against the marble floor, echoing like the steady beat of an drum rim. The lobby of the Harris, Cohan, and Beale building was deserted except for the security guard. He looked up from his console, nodded in her direction, and smiled. Alice didn't remember his name. The white tufts of hair sticking out below his billed cap were a stark contrast to his dark skin. In some ways, he reminded her of her father. Her father would work to have something productive to do. He complained about his job, looked forward to retirement, but had no plan to do anything. Why was it that so many people didn't plan for retirement.

She smiled back at the guard and headed for the elevator which always smelled faintly of old cigar smoke and body odor. She was glad to be alone as she rode up to the seventh floor.

"Hi, Alice," the receptionist said as Alice walked into the outer office of Results, a small subsidiary of HCB. "Here's your mail. I put your messages on your desk."

"Thanks, Catherine." Alice shuffled through the envelopes and then looked up. "Tell Eddie we'll need coffee and some sandwiches for the meeting. No doughnuts and no sweetrolls. And tell him to bring in some Cheesie Spread and crackers, too. It'll add a nice touch."

"Will do."

"Thanks." As Alice walked away, she looked back over her shoulder at the young blond woman at the reception desk wearing the telephone headset that looked like an earmuff with a sucker on a bent stick. "I really appreciate your help."

Catherine nodded and smiled.

Alice walked through the wood-paneled reception area. The two massive oak doors prevented clients from seeing the day-to-day chaos of people running late for appointments and wondering how to solve problems. She turned left into the corridor, past the small room housing the whirring and clunking office copy machine, to her tiny office half way down the narrow hall. A desk, a window, and a chair. Her office was one of the smallest, barely 8 by 8, created by shifting two moveable walls, stealing space from what were once two larger offices on both sides. She was thankful for the window. The sunlight streamed in between the buildings across the street, and one beam struck the miniature yellow rose plant on her desk, making it glow. There were offices that had no windows.

Setting her briefcase down in the doorway, she looked at the stack of yellow messages on the desk. "Doesn't it ever end?" she muttered. "I'll be all afternoon returning these damn calls. When am I gonna get some work done?" She looked out the window letting the sunlight warm her face as she decided on the easiest one to call first.

Catherine walked in and sat on the edge of the desk, smiling. She had another yellow message in her hand. "You had another message this morning," she whispered in her best I've-got-a-secret voice, "from Gregory Varonian. You know, Varonian and Varonian. His office called and asked for you by name. I didn't want to just leave it on your desk." She stood up, looking sideways at Alice. "Are you thinking of leaving us?"

The surprise that Gregory called on top of Catherine's suggestion that Alice might leave shocked Alice into speechlessness. She swallowed hard before she felt she could speak without squeaking.

"What're you talking about? I have no intention of leaving," she responded like someone still speaking after everyone else in a room had become quiet. The sound of her voice embarrassed them both. Alice felt warmth rising to her cheeks. She closed the blind, her fingers trembling. The entire incident of the weekend came rushing back.

"Don't be silly," she said, finally in command of her voice again, and speaking in what she hoped was a normal tone. "It just so happens that Greg and I went to college together. Probably something about the reunion."

"Really?" Her eyes opened wide and her eyebrows shot up. "What's he like? I heard he's a real bear to work for."

"I really don't know. It was years ago. And I never worked for him." Alice looked down at the messages on her desk. Her clipped tone told Catherine it was time to leave.

"Right. Well, the caller said it was important." She turned quickly, but stopped in the doorway and smiled. "Keep me informed, okay? You're one of the people that makes this job worth keeping." She turned and left.

That's all I need around here. Some stupid idea that I'm looking for another job.

She crumpled the message and threw it into the trash. Then she retrieved it and looked at it. She could feel the frustration creeping over her. "How can he do this to me?" she muttered. She clenched her fists and heard rapid breathing, as if she were another person. It was the other person who mechanically dialed the number.

"Varonian and Varonian will you hold please." said a voice in one breath. The tinny stereo soft rock music that played in only one ear gave Alice time to stuff her anger back into its small can and screw the lid on. She thumbed through other messages as she waited. The Cheesie Spread people had called to postpone the meeting until one o'clock, for which she was thankful. She could use the time to review the notes she had barely seen.

"May I help you?" said the same voice after a few seconds.

"Alice McBride returning Gregory Varonian's call."

"I'm sorry, but Mr. Varonian is in a meeting. May I take a message?"

Alice was silent for a moment, shaking her head and clamping her lips together. "Please tell him that I returned his call," she said curtly.

"What was your name again?"

"Just tell him Alice," she said abruptly. "He has the number. Extension is 425." She punched the button on her phone so hard her finger hurt.

Within five minutes, her phone rang.

"Alice McBride."

"Well, hello Alice," Gregory said, his voice oozing saccharine. "Glad you called." Then he changed to a normal conversational tone. "Sorry about that meeting shit, but you know what it's like trying to get some work done. I know you're busy, but I think we need to talk for a moment."

"What about?" she said, fearful of what might come next.

"About the weekend. I want to apologize."

Alice was relieved. His apology made her relax. A weight lifted from the back of her neck.

"You know me," he continued. "I'm not the macho Bruce Willis type."

"I'll admit, it did seem out of character. Even for you."

"Anyway, I was hoping we could have dinner sometime. I owe you that, at least.

Alice didn't respond right away. The weight started to return. She didn't want to have dinner with Gregory, but she also didn't want to antagonize him. He said 'sometime,' so she felt safe in saying yes. "Sure, that sounds fine. I'm sure Larry would like that."

"I was thinking of just the two of us, after work one day."

"Well, I don't think that's a good idea." She wanted to say 'Hell no,' but she decided to be polite.

"Hold on a second, Alice. I've got another call."

She knew that agreeing would give him more power over her. She was afraid. He seemed to have two personalities. If she had dinner with him, she didn't know which Gregory would show up: the monster at the cabin, or the polite man now on the phone. He had almost ruined her life once. She could never forget the crippling hurt, like the pain of a pebble punching unexpectedly into your bare heel. She had experienced the exhilaration of fear within trust. But he had let her crash.

The click told her he was back on the line.

"Look, Greg, I appreciate the apology. But what's past is past. It doesn't matter," she said in a bold, controlled voice. She stopped, waiting for him to say something, but the line was silent, so she continued. "Look, I've got the Cheesie Spread people coming here this afternoon, and…"

"I know," he cut her off. "But you'll be working late tonight on the Cheesie Spread account, won't you."

"Well, I didn't think so. The meeting shouldn't take more than a couple of hours." She paused and then tried to change the subject. "Are you interested in my package goods account? Jean said you had wanted it last year."

"Alice, get serious. If you're working late, I can take you to dinner and then drive you home. We're neighbors. Remember?"

She hesitated. She had the grinding feeling that something terrible was about to happen, like a storm she could feel before it comes, when the fine hair on her arms prickles. But it wasn't a storm. It was worse than that. A hurricane or tornado. She had a chilling premonition that a ruthless, destructive force would take her in its talons, and bear her relentlessly toward an aerie, to be torn apart by ravenous sharp beaks.

"Hey," Gregory continued. "It's just two old friends having dinner."

Right. Two old friends.

Her hesitancy made her wonder about herself. Should she confront him now, tell him no, risk his threats again? Or would she go like a lamb, meekly hoping that her feelings were wrong. She was standing on a line, and she had to jump across or stay where she was. In the back of her mind was the nagging reality, try-ing to claw its way to the front.

"I think I know how you feel, Greg. But we're both married now, and…" Her voice trailed off.

"All the more reason we ought to have dinner and get this thing out in the open. We need to talk about it like two mature adults."

"Greg, there's nothing to talk about." Alice sat up straight and put her knees together under her desk. "Besides," her voice rose to a higher pitch. She was grasping at a way out. "What're you going to tell Jean?" She wanted Gregory to back off, to make the decision for both of them. She was wavering, although her voice was firm. She knew if he persisted, she would give in.

"The truth, of course. That I'm having dinner with an old friend. She knows I stay in the city when I have an early morning meeting. It so happens that I have an eight o'clock meeting tomorrow."

"How convenient for you."

"Look, it's just dinner. Honest."

"What about your meeting?"

"If you want, I'll take you home and then drive back here. It's no big deal. You can take a cab if you'd rather. What do I have to say to make you agree?"

"Greg, I…"

"We could arm wrestle," he interrupted.

He knew the right buttons to push. They had jokingly arm wrestled when they lived together in college when they disagreed on which movie to see, or where to go for dinner. Alice had never won, although the laughter it caused had more than compensated for her losses, since the contests usually ended in bed. She made her decision.

"No arm wrestling, okay. Just dinner. And you can pay for my cab ride home." The queasiness in her stomach was the same feeling she got watching a child walk close to the observation windows of the Sears Tower. "I've got some things I've been carrying around for few years. You may not want to hear them."

"Pick you up at 6? We can go to Berghoff's. It's large and dark enough there. You'll feel safe."

"No. Not here. Meet you there at 6:30."

She considered how she would be able to tell Greg what she had felt when he abandoned her. She supposed it was possible to hate someone and eat dinner with him at the same time. She remembered reading about young women in the Nazi death camps, forced to go on "dates" with guards, to act like school-girls enjoying themselves. Always, always the unspoken threat, hanging by a hair, like the sword of Damocles.

CHAPTER 19

▼

The Berghoff, one of the oldest restaurants in downtown Chicago, offered clients a trade: the noise of Randolph Street for the somber quiet of the cavernous interior. Famous for its specials and its own beer and once frequented by the Chicago elite, it was now visited by conspiring businessmen whispering deals with other people's money.

They stood under the massive stained-glass partition. Their table was not quite ready, so they pushed their way to the ornate bar and ordered Berghoff Beer.

"Beer at the bar. Just like the old days," Gregory said.

"Except you didn't wear a suit, and we sure as hell didn't drink Berghoff."

"I can't even remember what they had on tap at McCabe's," he responded. Schlitz, I think. Or Bud."

"Did we come here to talk about the old days, Greg?" She paused, drew in her breath, and looked past him. Behind him, two people left a small table and she quickly walked to it and sat down. Greg pulled his chair to sit across from her. The noise and people annoyed her. Glasses clinking. The murmur of conversation. Men hovering over women. Women flirting. Back at the bar, she saw a short-skirted gray business suit move ever so slightly to a position between the legs of a seated navy blue suit. Married people don't stand like that. Only single people or those trying to move up the corporate bedpost. She wondered how many people were there cheating on their spouses, and she felt embarrassed. She looked at Greg, and decided to be blunt. "This is very awkward. What do you want from me?"

"That's pretty direct. Just to talk. Find out things how are."

"What do you mean 'How things are'? You know how things are."

"You know what I mean. Talk to you. Alone."

"We could have talked at the cabin. We were alone there."

"I made a mistake. So sue me. I apologized."

"Where do you want to start?" She leaned back and sipped her beer, the sweet smell of tobacco smoke reminding her of the last time they had a drink and dinner together.

It had not been at McCabe's, but at The Hillside, a restaurant where college students took their visiting parents. They had wanted a quiet evening to talk about plans for after graduation. They were going to work for Gregory's father and Gregory was going to paint. He had plans for at least seven canvasses in addition to the three he was currently working on. But all that had ended abruptly.

"At the end. What the hell went wrong?"

Alice felt stunned. She thought he might be sarcastic, but the look on his face told her he wasn't.

"What went wrong? Duhh," Alice gave a half laugh. "You telling me you have no idea?" She paused, leaned forward and looked at his face. "You sure you want to hear this?" Shaking her head, she was struck that an otherwise intelligent man could be as dense as the table. "Let me give you the abridged version. You decided to fuck a certain model, as I recall, which fucked up our relationship." She grinned at him, and then softened the grin to a smile, wondering if he'd be able to decipher the irony. "Then, of course, there was the abortion. But I'm sure you were too busy, what with finals and graduation. And all."

He closed his eyes and rubbed them. "You don't know how sorry I was. The whole thing was a big mistake. I realized that as soon as you moved out."

"But you stayed with her. You married her, for crissake. It couldn't have been that much of a mistake."

"An arm ornament, my dad calls her. She looks good wherever we go. She says the right things, does the right things, but there's nothing up there," he said touching his head.

Alice felt the slap as keenly now as she had then. He traded the blunt Polish college girl from working-class North Chicago for the slick Chicago model. Her stomach tightened and for a moment, she thought she might vomit. She sipped her beer and forced herself to swallow. "Too bad," she managed to say through tight lips. "I suppose I should be flattered. But don't sell her short. She's not as dumb as you think."

Why am I defending this woman? I ought to hate her, but I don't.

"I knew what she was from the start. She knows what I tell her. She was after the money. But after you left, what was I to do?"

"You've got that a little backward," she said sitting up straight. "You're the one who broke things off, remember."

"Does that really matter now?"

Gregory waved when he heard his name called. The Maitre D' told them their table was ready, and they followed a balding, white-haired portly waiter in a tux back into the restaurant to a table near the huge stained glass windows. The red and gold glass reflected the light, casting an eerie shadow on the table.

They ate in silence. Alice ordered lamb, and Gregory ordered the goulash, a specialty of the house. She picked at the food, hardly tasting the chops. She was afraid of her anger, afraid of the silence, afraid of everything unsaid. Conflicting feelings pounded through her chest, but she kept her head down and looked at her food. She sliced a piece of chop, thinking that once she and Gregory had sliced off pieces of the same dream.

Before they broke up, she had visions of what their life together would be like. After they broke up, it pulsed behind her eyes, like a fever. The shards of that first shattered dream had stayed with her as an undercurrent of pain, like seeing the warm town of her youth disappearing in the rear view mirror as she drove away to college for the first time. After the abortion, she had started envisioning his agonizing death. She stood over him and laughed at his unendurable pain. She had often tried to fantasize a life with their child, but couldn't without remembering the anguish of the abortion.

The silence grew oppressive. Finally, Greg broke the deadlock.

"Look, Alice, I told myself I wouldn't say this, but I've got to. I think I'm still in love with you. I thought I had pushed it to the back burner of my mind, but the moment I saw you at the store, the feelings came flooding back."

"And so you almost raped me?" she said, looking at his face. In the weak light, he looked evil. "Is that what this dinner is all about?"

"I said I'm sorry. Things got out of hand at the cabin. You know me better than that. You know I wouldn't do anything to hurt you."

"Maybe not. But right now it's all I can do not to pick up that knife and stab you again. I gave up wishing for what I didn't have years ago, wishing for the years we won't spend together. And I'm also in love. With a wonderful guy who works hard and wants a family, same as I do. And I wouldn't do anything to hurt him. Not anything."

"That's good. I'm glad you wouldn't hurt him. I hardly know him, and I wouldn't want to hurt him either." He dropped his fork into his plate with a clank and looked straight at her, waiting for a response.

Alice felt caught, like a bug pierced on a pinning tray, wriggling helplessly, but unable to touch the surface. She didn't need to ask what he was hinting at. Gregory made everything perfectly clear.

"I want you as passionately as ever. And I know we'll see each other again. But I'm going to get you home because that's what I promised. Life is strange, isn't it? Who would have thought we'd ever be having dinner in such a sensuous atmosphere."

CHAPTER 20

▼

He gave the cabby a hundred dollars to take Alice back to Lake Forest. She sat in the back of the taxi in silence, a large wad of tissue in her hand to dab at her tears which flowed freely down her cheeks. Alice's treachery had not yet sprouted, its seed still buried in her bosom. Her silent tears provided sufficient moisture for the seed to take root. She had no idea it was starting to grow, nor did she know that to nurture the tree would dry up her heart. The driver took her to the train station, where she got into her car, rolled the windows down, and hoped the cool night air would calm her. The sky was cloudy and ominous, and the air was heavy with moisture. It was after 11, but she sat in her car for several minutes before she drove home.

Larry was in bed, asleep. He always rose early to be at the garage before 7 AM. She looked at him, so relaxed when he slept. All the lines in his face smoothed, and he didn't move. For him, there were no problems. She wrinkled her forehead, clamped her teeth, and shook her head, wondering what decisions she would be forced to make in the next few days.

CHAPTER 21

▼

When Alice awoke the next morning, Larry was already in the shower. She closed her eyes in the embracing the warmth of half-sleep, and listened to the music of the water against the shower door. The splashing took her back to the waterfalls at the sacred pools in Maui, where she and Larry had spent their honeymoon. She savored the memory, aching for the ardent intimacy they had once known.

Larry's voice startled her as he walked into the room. "That must have been some meeting last night, Babe," he said as he ruffled a towel softly through his hair.

"What do you mean?" She fearfully heard Catherine's voice saying, "I'm sorry, but Miz McBride has left for the day would you like to leave a message on her voice mail?" It had taken days of explaining to his silent stares that she really didn't remember Gregory from college.

"It's been a long time since I went to bed before you got home." He turned and went back into the bathroom to brush his hair. "My head is really pounding."

"How many beers did you have?"

"Al came by to watch the game and we finished off a couple six packs."

"You mean you finished off a couple of six packs. What'd Al have? Two beers?" She looked at the once rippled stomach that was beginning to soften.

"Don't worry about me, Babe," he said patting his stomach. "I'll work it off. That's one good thing about the kind of work I do. Good as working out in some fancy club. And it don't cost me nothing."

"Larry, there's something we've got to talk about." Alice sat up in bed, pulling the sheet over her breasts and tucking it under her armpits.

"Here it comes. Now what?" Their disagreements were like boxing matches. The punches were imaginary, unlike Larry's hard-drinking, Irish grandfather, who had used real punches to end differences. Larry put up his guard. His method of solving problems was to retreat into silence and drink.

"That's what I want to know," she said. "What's the problem? We haven't made love for weeks. We made love more often before we were married."

Please, she pleaded silently. *Don't disappear. Do something. Get into bed with me and hold me.*

He slipped on his green work shirt. "Jesus Christ. What the hell do you want from me? You know I been going crazy at the shop."

"I thought you wanted to have a family. I'm 31, and I don't want to be raising kids when I'm 50."

"Well, if you were home in the evening," he said to her reflection in the mirror, "it might be different."

"Yeah, right. Once a month or so I work late. Let me know when you plan to stop drinking beer and falling asleep in your chair."

"Shit, what the hell do you know." He put on his work pants, his face distorted in a scowl. He sat at the foot of the bed and his voice became soft. "I'm sorry. You know I love you, and things haven't been real good lately. Too much on my head. I got the payments on the garage, the tools, the trucks, Eddie wants a raise. Maybe it's more than I can handle."

"Larry, that part I understand, but you know that's not the problem. I think the real problem is you're afraid when there's nothing to be afraid of. You really need to go in for that sperm count the doctor recommended."

He stood up. "I told you I'm not going to jerk off into some goddamn bottle. There's nothing wrong with me. Maybe you're the one who can't get pregnant. What makes you think it's me that's got the problem?"

"Because I already had a test."

He shook his head. "Ah, what's the use talking," he said looking at his watch. "I'll see you tonight." In a few moments, Alice heard the front door close and his truck start up. Then she was alone. In a few moments, sobs wrenched her. She pushed her face in the pillow, drenching it in tears.

"What am I going to do," she lamented, punching her fist into the pillow. "Thank God Larry didn't know enough to ask what test I'd had."

Are there times when telling a lie is better that telling the truth? What if telling the truth hurts someone and telling a lie would prevent that person from being hurt. Maintaining the lie I might hurt only myself, and maybe not very much.

If only she could appease Gregory in some way and get him off her back. Gregory had her in his power. There would be no end.

She wiped her eyes and headed for the shower. *Why can't he just go in for the test. Why does he equate sperm count with masculinity?*

As she dressed, she only had time for a cup of coffee and a muffin on the train as she went over her notes for the Friday morning brain-storming. The sound of thunder rumbled in the distance. She saw gray clouds blocking the sun, turning the day into night.

CHAPTER 22

▼

Alice arrived at work and went directly to her office. Her mind was clogged with personal thoughts that blocked her creative conduit. In the narrow corridor, Alice passed her friend, Sarah Dotson without speaking.

"Hey, Alice, anybody home?"

Alice stopped. Sarah had been Alice's mentor and the two women were close friends. In the past, Alice would have talked to Sarah about her unhappiness, but now she hesitated. It was one thing to complain about an insensitive husband, but who would believe what was going on with Gregory Varonian. Alice believed her complaints would look foolish. Her problems were her own. She was also afraid Sarah would tell her to do what Alice couldn't do: tell the truth.

"Sorry, Sarah. I'm in a fog today. Problems. I'm really somewhere else."

"What happened? Sarah's smile faded quickly when Alice looked at her.

As they stood in the hall, Catherine handed Alice a message and smiled. "It seems Mr. Gregory Varonian wants you to call him. Again." She said it just loud enough to make sure Sarah heard. The surprise on Sarah's face was unmistakable.

"Thanks, Catherine," said Alice, her voice as loud as Catherine's. "I'll have to call him later. I've got to meet with the creative team on the Cheezie Spread account. We've got some real problems to work out."

"Good old FCS?" grinned Catherine.

"Whatever. Call Bob and Theresa and tell them I'm setting up a meeting for Monday morning. If we don't get this baby moving, we're in deep doo-doo."

"How 'bout lunch?" asked Sarah, quietly. "I've still got a good ear."

"Thanks, but I don't know. This isn't what it appears to be."

"Twelve-thirty? Sounds like you need to talk, friend." Sarah smiled in a sympathetic way that seemed to encompass Alice's pain. Sarah was too good a friend to reject.

"Okay. 12:30."

"Good. Now I've got to see what I can do about this." Sarah waved a sheaf of papers over her head.

"Thanks." Alice went to her office where she ate a few saltine crackers. Her stomach calmed, but her head still spun.

The team for Cheezie Spread account had not come up with creative new ways to use the product. At the end of the last meeting, Bob said, "There are just so many things you can do with Cheezie Spread without getting obscene."

Alice had playfully suggested Cheezie Spread wrestling. "Like mud wrestling, except you can eat the medium." The insane suggestions broke the tension they were under.

"Or it could be warmed and used as a sexual lubricant," Teresa laughed.

After that, the team had taken to calling the account FCS, their humorous acronym for Fucking Cheezie Spread. The acronym had been picked up by others in the office.

CHAPTER 23

▼

"Why are men so scared of their image," Alice told Sarah at lunch. "Wouldn't it be so much easier to deal with the problem and get the sperm test?"

"Well, that's because they're men. We women would never do that. Would we?"

She had a wry sense of humor, and Alice's mind wasn't functioning well.

That's what I'm doing with Gregory. Hoping the problem will go away.

"I think the doctor might have better luck with Larry, Alice."

"I guess I worry that Larry can't have children, even though he wants them as bad as I do.

"You know for sure he's the problem?"

"Yeah. I had a fertility test," she lied, smiling at the thought. "I'm fertile."

"What about adoption? You know how easy it is, especially if you take a mixed ethnic child.

"Are you kidding, Sarah? Larry with a dark-skinned child? It's not that he's prejudiced, but he's already made it clear he doesn't want someone else's mistake."

"In some ways, that's understandable. He still drinking?"

"Yeah. More than he should. But at least he sticks to beer and mostly drinks at home. Maybe I'm expecting too much."

For years, Alice thought her mother and her father had a master-slave relationship. Her father would come home from work, wash up, and flop in his chair. Her mother would stop what she was doing, bring him a beer and the newspaper, and then finish preparing dinner. Although her mother worked part-time as a clerk at Eisenberg's Clothing Store, she never let her hours interfere with what she called her "household duties." It was as if her father was the earth and her mother the moon, revolving by choice around the greater body, allowing herself only heatless, reflected light.

When Alice married Larry, she began to understand happiness is neither the absence of sadness, nor the distance between the two. It is the difference between what is expected and what occurs. When one expects little and gets more, happiness results. Her grandmother had been beaten by her grandfather. Alice's mother was happy that she had married a man who was hardworking, never drank to excess, and treated her with what she considered respect.

"Well, no one's happy all the time," said Sarah. "Except maybe people in mental institutions. In a way, they're lucky. They don't know where they are."

"They live in their own worlds. We, on the other hand, have to live in reality. Now that's crazy."

They both laughed.

Walking back to the office, Sarah asked, "What's the situation with Gregory Varonian?"

"Greg and I went to college together, and he suggested I might fit in at his agency. But don't even hint about that. There's no way I'd work for him."

"I don't think ever I told you, but I used to work there. Years ago, before Gregory even started there."

"You worked for the old man?"

"I was there when Gregory started. It was even before he graduated from college. There was some tension between the old man and him when he took up with a model."

"What happened?" Alice hoped she didn't appear too anxious to hear another side of the story.

"I'm not sure. I came here about six months after Gregory graduated and joined the firm. I heard they eventually got married. She was a real knockout, and had brains to match. She could have run that whole place if she'd wanted to. I got to like her."

Alice nodded and kept silent. It was becoming hard to dislike Jean.

After lunch, Alice called returned Gregory's call.

"Alice. Nice to hear from you. I've got to go to New York for a few days on this KFC thing. I'll call you when I get back."

"Greg, why are you doing this to me?"

"Because I need to." Then the connection went dead.

Alice felt she was being cut into a jigsaw puzzle. If some of the pieces got lost, she'd never be able to put herself together.

CHAPTER 24

▼

On Saturday Alice made a turkey, along with real mashed potatoes, carrots with brown sugar, and home-made cranberry sauce. And a strawberry pie, Larry's favorite. She called Michael, Larry's brother, who worked as a detective in Waukegan. Eight years older, Michael lived in the Castle Crest subdivision on the north side of Waukegan less than twenty miles away, although the two brothers seldom saw each other. Growing up, Michael had taken care of Larry and still tried to give the younger man advice. He thought Larry should have gone to technical school instead of learning to be a mechanic the hard way. Michael had completed two years of college and disliked Larry's drinking, while Larry often bragged that he was lucky he was to have graduated from high school. Larry called Michael's advice-giving the older brother disease.

When Larry came home from work, the turkey was in the oven, sending its aroma out like a courier bearing pleasant news. The strawberry pie was cooling on the counter, its sweet, tangy fragrance mixed with the smell of garlic bread stuffing. She hoped the meal and ambiance would put Larry in a relaxed mood, maybe even romantic.

"What's going on here?" His eyes were glassy, and he spread his arms in an exaggerated gesture. "We having company or something?"

"Just thought I'd like to make a nice dinner."

"Thass wonderful. I mean it. Really wonderful." He walked to his large gray chair and flopped down in it.

"Michael's coming over. But it sounds like you've already had your company. You take everyone go over to The Lamplight again?" Alice, intentionally stood in front of the TV.

"Yup. My regular Saturday afternoon workers' conference." He picked up the remote. "Hey, don't stand there. I can't turn on the TV." He paused. "The Bulls are playing the Knicks." He grinned at Alice. "I don't suppose I could get you to bring me a beer, could I?"

Alice walked through the kitchen and continued outside to sit on the porch steps. She hunched forward, head in her hands, elbows on her knees.

A large blackbird looked down at her and laughed from a large maple tree. Across the street, behind the large two-story white house facing hers, was the ravine. In the spring, it had water trying to find its way through a maze of channels and drain tiles to Lake Michigan. She wished a raging flood would carry her away. A childhood memory of a missed sleepover flashed through her mind.

When she was thirteen, Alice decided to cook dinner. The potatoes turned out dry, and the meat was overcooked. Only the peas were edible.

"You can eat this shit," her father had bulled at her and stormed out of the house.

After her mother came home, he returned, smelling of beer and garlic. When Alice tried to leave the house quietly, he stopped her.

"Where the hell you going?" he shouted. "Don't you have things to do?"

"It's Saturday night," Alice said. "There's a sleepover at Susan's."

"Well, you're not going anywhere!" He believed that life was hard and only those who were harder survived.

There was no point arguing. "It's like trying to shape granite with your fingers," her mother always said.

CHAPTER 25

▼

Larry was asleep in his chair when Michael arrived. There were six empty beer cans on the floor next to next to him. Michael walked through the kitchen and joined Alice on the back porch.

"Up to his usual, I see."

Alice threw her arms around his neck. Tears glistened in her eyes.

"Oh, shit, Mike," she half spoke, half sobbed. "Oh, shit."

She undid her arm. Michael was an inch shorter than Larry, but with the same boyish, freckled good looks.

"You look tired, Mike. Something wrong?"

"Nah. Been working too many hours. Getting so I can't tell the good guys from the bad guys any more." He shook his head. "Hey, the house smells fantastic. I don't think I've had a meal like this since," he paused. "Well, since Cindy left me. What can I do to help? I'm starved."

They returned to the kitchen.

"Well, so much for a family dinner tonight," said Alice.

Michael sat at the kitchen table while Alice sliced the turkey and set the slices on a serving plate.

"What's going on in your life, Mike?"

"Not much. The usual. Got an interesting homicide, though. I shouldn't talk about it."

Alice brought three plates to the table. Each was filled with meat, mashed potatoes, carrots, and cranberry sauce. She set one at the place where Larry should be sitting.

"You going to wake him?" asked Michael.

"God damn him," she said. "It'll be sitting right there when he decides to get up."

Michael laughed. "I told you that you married the wrong guy. You should have married me."

"Well, you were already married when I met Larry, remember?"

"Oh, yeah." He smiled, his eyes sparkling. "I forgot. That must have been Cindy."

Alice punched him on the shoulder.

"Y'know, I never did understand what you saw in him. Aside from the fact that underneath his grime and booze, there's a decent guy trying to squeeze out."

"I suppose. But it's getting harder and harder to remember that."

"He's digging himself quite a hole. If he gets in deep enough, he may never get out. Just like the old man." Michael kept his eyes on the food as he spoke. "And he was a mean son-of-a-bitch when he drank. At least Larry doesn't take after him in that way. Does he?"

"No. He just gets quiet."

Michael asked Alice about her work, and they both laughed when she told the story of FCS.

"What's the homicide?

"A lawyer was killed in a hit and run accident. Pretty gruesome. The body was carried about 200 feet before it was thrown from the car."

"Yeah. It was in the News-Sun. They made it sound like an accident, not a homicide."

"Well, we got a suspect, but I don't think we'll be able to do anything. Some of us think the lawyer got what he deserved, but it's not my place to judge."

"You think he killed the guy on purpose? How could he could do something like that?"

"We think we know the motive. The problem is we don't have any hard evidence."

"But eventually you'll get him, won't you?"

"Maybe. Maybe not. The case'll stay open until something happens, which may be never. We'll go after the ones we can solve."

Alice put her fork down and looked at her brother-in-law. "You mean there are people who get away with murder?"

"You been watching too much TV. They always get the killer. Just when it looks like there's no evidence, an eye witness turns up. But this's real life. There are cases the police can't do anything about. They get buried under glowing reports."

"So you ignore the tough problems and tackle the easy ones. Everyone looks good on paper?"

"Hey, wait a minute. We do the best we can with the resources we have. It all comes down to money. We're not going to let serial killers or rapists get away. Or cop-killers. But if this guy did it, he killed the lawyer who wiped out his family in a drunk driving accident."

Alice didn't respond. She wondered how her life would change if Larry were dead. Then she thought about the times she had wished Gregory dead. She didn't think she could actually kill him.

"Hey, you thinking about someone you want dead?" He nodded his head in the direction of Larry. "Just divorce him. It's easier. And a hell-of-a lot cheaper."

Michael offered to help clean up, but Alice refused.

She walked Michael to the door. Larry still slept, unmoving.

"He's going to have one hell-of-a-stiff neck tomorrow. Let me know if there's anything I can do." Then he left.

Alice cleaned the kitchen, leaving Larry's plate of food on the table, and went upstairs to read in bed. About two in the morning, Alice felt him crawling into bed.

The next morning, anger smoldered like glowing pine knot embers, but she said nothing. She made coffee and ate some toast. Larry said nothing about the crusty, dried food still on the table. He took a cup of coffee and went into the living room, and turned on the TV.

Alice started to vacuum. It was either push herself or get the baseball bat from the garage and put Larry's head into left field. She imagined showing Michael the hole in the window made by Larry's head.

"What's got into you?" He glanced up from a football game, beer in hand. "I'm getting winded just watching you."

"It's those new vitamins I'm taking," she shouted over the noise of the vacuum. "They're supposed to boost my energy level. I guess they're working. Oh, and Michael said hello when he was here yesterday. I guess you missed him."

CHAPTER 26

▼

On Monday, Alice jumped every time the phone on her desk rang. Gregory could be on the other end of the line. She walked to the coffee room, and her hand shook as she poured a cup of coffee.

"Alice, what the hell's going on? You're totally frazzled," said Sarah touching her friend's shoulder.

"It's this Cheesie Spread account," she lied. "And on top of that, Larry and I had a big fight this weekend," she added, hoping a little truth would be a blanket. "We need to go for counseling." She went back to her office without saying another word.

Gregory called on Wednesday afternoon. "Hi, Alice. Just got back last night." He managed to sound pleasant, as if this were a happy social call.

"So?" she said. She imagined herself to be an ice cube.

"Well, we landed the KFC account for the midwest. Now we've got to produce."

She said nothing.

He continued, "But that's not what I called about." His voice became hushed. "Jean's going back to New York for a while. Her father's sick, and it may be cancer, so she wants to be with him."

"Sorry. What does it have to do with me?" She felt a vise squeezing her breath away.

That evening, Gregory took Alice to dinner at Berghoff's again. This time he ordered manhattans for both of them. Alice drank hers quickly and began to feel relaxed. Gregory immediately ordered her another, which she finished as the meal was being served.

Alice drank to rub out the edges of her pain, and alcohol is a brilliant, if temporary, eraser. She consumed a third manhattan during the meal, and another after. She had difficulty standing, and Gregory had to help her to his car.

After driving to his home in Lake Forest with her asleep, he half carried her up the stairs to his studio above the six car garage. It was one vast room with three large skylights. He took off his shoes as he entered, as if he were sneaking in, although there was no need for silence. He motioned for her to do the same as he supported her, one arm around her back and one hand under her arm. Bracing herself against him, she complied. Near the door was a small wooden chair, in which Alice sat, her head hanging, her shoulders slumped.

A partially finished canvas leaned against a wooden folding partition, a half finished aerial scene showing Chicago skyscrapers on the right and Lake Michigan on the left.

"That's looking south from the Hancock Building. Acrylic." he said walking toward it.

Alice looked back toward the doorway. Something told her she ought to leave, but her body was no longer controlled by her mind. She glanced toward the painting, mumbled something, and then looked down, motionless.

"You don't have to sit like there a zombie. Come on," said Gregory. He grasped her arm. His strong hand pulled her to her feet, turning her around and around, finally to face him. He held her arms at her sides. As he bent down to kiss her, she turned her face away.

"Don't do this to me Greg." Her voice was plaintive, but tinged with rusted iron. "Take me home, and we'll forget all about it." Her hands felt moist. Her body was limp. She sat back down, unable to move.

"Go home? To your greasy mechanic? The party hasn't started yet."

"Please, Greg. You said you loved me once."

"I know what. If you want to go home, call Larry. Tell him to come and pick you up. He knows how to get here, doesn't he? The phone's there." He pointed to a small table.

Alice didn't move. Her tears flowed.

"Now don't start that. It's a little late."

Her freedom had turned into shackles of lies. There was nothing for her to do but acquiesce, like when she was a child.

"We've done it all before," Gregory continued. "Remember the times we just couldn't wait to jump into bed together?"

"That was another time, another place. We've got real lives now." Her voice came from a place within where she had not been for a long time.

"Oh, yes. Reality. But yours is a movie about a man who is in charge and a woman," he paused, "who's married to the wrong man. Sort of *A Wonderful Life* with a twist."

He touched her cheek with the back of his fingers and then put his palm against her face. She wanted to pull away, but knew it was useless. A frost came over her body, a numbness spreading down from her shoulders to her breasts and stomach, down to her calves. Her legs trembled. She had no control over herself, but she was aware of everything that happened. When she felt his hands unbuttoning her blouse, she swung her fist in slow motion, catching his shoulder.

"Easy now," he said. "I don't want to tear anything. You'd have a hard time explaining ripped clothes, wouldn't you?" Gregory removed Alice's blouse and bra, and took off his tie and shirt. He helped her stand, and told her to remove her skirt and panties.

"I want to see if you've changed in the last six years."

Robot-like, she obeyed, doing what she was told. She stood before him, naked, waiting for his next order, totally submissive to his requests. She was no longer drunk. She had effectively removed herself. Her body was there, but Alice was gone.

From behind the partition, Gregory dragged a futon, and unrolled it on the floor.

"Lie down there," he said, standing to remove his pants. He pulled down his jockey shorts and kneeled between her legs, grabbing her ankles and placing them on his shoulders. Placing his hands on her hips, he pulled her toward him and entered her. Alice winced slightly, a physical response. Holding her knees, Gregory leaned into her, rocking back and forth until he exploded in release.

CHAPTER 27

▼

Three days later, Gregory called Alice at work, telling her to meet him at The Drake, an elegant hotel where he often stayed when he had early morning meetings. Alice refused and hung up. He called Catherine and had her deliver a message to call him.

"He offered you a job, didn't he?" Catherine said.

Alice shook her head. "He's helping me plan a surprise birthday party for Larry. I'm not leaving here."

She dialed Gregory's number. "How long is this going to go on? Haven't you humiliated me enough?"

"Humiliated? Now why should you feel humiliated? I didn't force you to do anything that you never did before."

"What happened was a terrible mistake. For both of us. And if you keep calling me, you'll be as sorrier than I will."

"Is that a threat? You're in no position to threaten me."

"I made a mistake. I won't make another one."

"You'll call me when you're ready."

Six weeks later, she called Gregory. "I need to talk to you."

"I heard things aren't going well at Results. Did you want to discuss a new job? Or will it be just two college lovers enjoying another nice dinner."

"We'll start with dinner." She knew this was the last dinner they would ever have alone.

CHAPTER 28

Alice met Gregory at the Star of Siam, a Thai restaurant near the overpass on Illinois Street. She wondered why she had ever thought him handsome. His dark hair seemed greasy, and his face now looked pockmarked and sleazy.

When the waiter came by, Alice ordered a caffeine-free diet coke.

He smiled and ordered a Singha beer. "What's the matter," Gregory joked. "Larry put you on the wagon?"

Alice wanted to slap him. She had been lying to Larry and trying to make it up to him in ways he didn't understand. She was climbing a mountain of deception. And here was Gregory, ready to push her off, and force her to take Larry with her as she crashed her way down.

Their dinners were served. Alice looked at the long serving spoon in her bowl of steaming rice and vegetables. Holding the spoon by the tip of the handle, she scooped up a few vegetables, and put them on her plate.

"I'm pregnant," she said as she spooned pieces of meat onto the vegetables.

"What?"

"I said I'm pregnant." She repeated the words slowly.

This time he said nothing. He slowly looked at the ceiling, took a breath, and then looked back at her.

"Well, what're you going to do?"

"My decision? Again?"

"What can I do?"

Alice leaned over the table, half standing. "What'll you do when everyone finds out this is your child?"

"I think you've got that a bit twisted. You first have to prove it's mine. And you have to explain how you got pregnant in the first place."

"You rotten son-of-a-bitch."

"How do you know it's mine? I mean, what about Larry?"

The heat and noise of the restaurant pressed. Alice started to sweat. She could hear the shupe-a, shupe-a, shupe-a of blood shushing through her ears as she gripped the edge of the table.

In a quick movement, she pushed her uneaten meal at Gregory. Both meals, soup, water, and tea spilled on his lap and onto the floor. She stormed toward the door. Gregory tried to avoid the waterfall pouring over the edge of the table, but his lap and shirt were covered with vegetables, chicken, lemon grass, and mushrooms. Three waiters rushed to the table when they heard the sound of the stainless steel soup pot clanging on the tile floor, followed by the tinkle of shattering glass. He handed the first waiter a hundred dollar bill, and rushed after Alice, grabbing her arm as she reached the door.

"You're crazy," he shouted at her.

She pulled her arm away and stomped outside. Everyone in the restaurant was looking at them. Gregory followed her, glad to be out of sight of the patrons and staff.

Turning the corner and walking toward Grand Avenue, the cool night air made her breathe deeply. Gregory caught up to her again at the corner.

"I think I need to have a talk with Larry," he repeated, a bit more breathless.

"Have a talk with anyone you want. Tell the whole fucking world. Put it on WGN. I don't give a shit. I made a terrible mistake, and I'm through." She stepped down the high curb and started across the street.

"You're making another mistake," he yelled at her back as he stood on the sidewalk. In the middle of Grand Avenue, she turned slowly and walked back toward him. He sneared as he folded his arms across his chest. Because the curb was high and his arms were folded, he didn't see her fist, or her right arm pull back. All he felt was pain, as her fist slammed into his groin. He saw darkness sprinkled with bright lights as he gasped in agony and slowly fell to his knees, then stumbled off the curb. He lay on his back in the oil, grease, dirt, and old newspapers, his knees raised to his chest, his hands holding the area that screamed in sharp pain.

Alice bent over him. "Listen to me, you piece of shit. I realized something. You can't condemn me without condemning yourself. And Jean will tear you to shreds. So tell anyone you want. I handled this before, and I'll handle it again."

She waved her hand and a taxi U-turned. Slamming the door, she hoped Gregory would be crushed by one of the city's garbage trucks.

She decided to let Larry to think the baby was his. After all, she was barely five weeks into the pregnancy. She was glad now that Larry had tried to make love to her when he had been drunk. Larry always wanted children. Especially a son to carry on his name. He claimed he could be a good father. It was simple, he said. He would think of what his father did, and he would do the opposite.

CHAPTER 29

▼

Alice was four months pregnant before she saw Gregory again. Although he and Larry sometimes met for a beer, she refused any social engagement that involved Gregory. Her pregnancy was a convenient excuse. In November, Larry got tickets to the yearly auto show at McCormick Place from a friend at the Mercedes/Jaguar dealer where he once worked.

"Think I'll call Greg and invite him and Jean to go with us to the auto show at McCormick Place. I know how he likes cars, especially new expensive ones."

"I don't know if I'm up for it."

"They're unveiling the new Caddy Sunday. Make a day of it. We can have dinner in the city."

"I want to spend Sunday at home, Lar. It's my only day to relax. And the way I've been feeling, I just want to sit with my feet up." She knew it would be a tense, upsetting day.

"C'mon, Alice, some of the new designs and engines'll blow you away. It'll be fun. You need to get some exercise, anyway."

"What I need is rest and relaxation, not crowds looking at cars that they can't afford to buy."

And spending an afternoon with Jean. Oh, by the way, your husband got me pregnant. Again. Just like he did seven years ago. Isn't that fascinating?

"What's the problem?" he asked.

"I'll tell you what the problem is. You'll want to stop and have a few drinks, and I can't drink. Or someone will suggest dinner, and the thought of eating makes me want to vomit. You'll enjoy the day, and I'll have a sore back. Remember when we went to the ball game? Who watched the game and who spent the time in the bathroom throwing up?"

"It's not going to be like that again. I promise. If you start feeling bad, we'll leave and come right home."

She understood his promises. They were like a child's promise not to get dirty in a muddy yard. But it was useless to argue. Like her mother, Alice knew the energy cost to refuse was too great.

Rather than driving and trying to park at McCormick Place, they took the train into the city. Larry promised his drinking would not cause any embarrassment, but Alice worried. Along with her pregnancy, his drinking weighed as heavily as her guilt.

Arriving at the show, Larry and Greg left Alice and Jean seated at the coffee plaza together. Alice felt pressure to be cautious when talking about her past.

"Where'd you live at Northern?" asked Jean.

"I shared a house with another woman on Haish." Alice wanted to speak only about the recent past or about childhood.

"Do you miss modeling? I'd think the excitement would be hard to give up," Alice finished her iced decaf cappuccino, and the two women walked toward the stairs to the second floor.

"Excitement? You mean drudgery and hard work. Whoever says slavery is dead hasn't been a model. The only difference is if you're hot, you get to sell yourself, and you can make big money. The rest of us get sold like sheep to the highest bidder. And the agency gets the big money."

"I didn't think it was that bad."

"And the guys hitting on you," continued Jean, without listening to Alice. "Give me a break. They think that because you're a model you'll do anything with anyone. I couldn't wait to get out of that rat-race. When I got the chance to work for Nishan's agency, I jumped at it. The potential wasn't as great, but it was a good weekly paycheck, and I could pay my bills. That's where I met Greg."

As if I didn't know.

"What about you?" asked Jean.

Alice talked about growing up in North Chicago. When her father had first moved there, it was a strongly ethnic community, Polish and Lithuanian. The big draw was Abbott Labs.

"People either worked for Abbott or wanted to. I remember my father telling me about a janitor who retired with over a quarter of a million in Abbott stock. He'd started with Abbott out of high school and had worked there for 42 years."

"How about your father."

"He'll be okay when he retires. At least financially. But I don't know what he'll do with his life. He's lost when the TV breaks down. I told him he needs a hobby, but he still sees me as a little girl who doesn't know a thing about what he calls 'the real world'."

They met Larry and Gregory and ate lunch. Jean insisted the four spend the afternoon together. Alice was pleased. If she had suggested it, Larry would have found some reason not to. She started to like Jean even more.

They walked across the bridge to the bar in the hotel. Larry finished two beers before Alice had sipped half her diet cola. Gregory and Jean had martinis with two olives.

"Man, I was thirsty," said Larry, ordering a third beer. "There was nothing to drink there except coffee and sodas."

"Why don't we head for home to have dinner," Alice suggested "It's early, but by the time we get there, it'll be dinner time. Besides, it's already been a long day for me. I need to stretch out and put my feet up."

"I've got an idea," Gregory said, ignoring Alice's comments. "Ever been to the Como Inn for dinner. It used to be one of the top places in the city. The food's still great. We can have dinner and still get an early train home."

"Sounds good to me," said Larry.

The Como Inn had kept its reputation for fine dining in an area that had deteriorated. The cab ride took them past houses and buildings that had once been inhabited by Chicago's well-to-do middle class. Now there were broken windows and graffiti-covered brick.

After they were seated and had ordered dinner, Larry suggested they go to a club after dinner where they could dance. "I always love dancing with my beautiful wife. Don't you think she's beautiful, Greg?"

Gregory looked at Alice and then at Jean. "Of course, she's beautiful, Larry. Especially now."

"Cut it out, you two. I'm tired, my legs hurt, and I don't feel like dancing. I feel like going home."

"As beautiful as when she was in college? Or don't you remember." Alice forgot how tired she was and sat up. As a waiter passed by, Larry grabbed his arm and ordered another beer.

"Maybe we ought to wait until the food comes, Lar," said Alice quietly, hesitant to take charge. "We haven't eaten much all day."

"Hey, you don't need to tell me what to do. Right, Greg? I'll bet Jean don't tell you what to do. Do you Jean?"

Gregory just shrugged and said nothing. Jean stared at her martini. When the food arrived, everyone ate silently.

The tension for Alice bordered on violent. Food sat undigested in her stomach. She could feel it surging, blocked at the end of her esophagus. She hardly spoke. Halfway through the dinner, she excused herself and almost ran to the ladies' room, where she vomited what little she had eaten. Jean appeared, wet a napkin, and handed it to Alice.

"Feeling better?"

"Yeah, a little."

"You know, you're lucky, being pregnant. I'm not sure I'd want a kid, even if I could have one."

"Can't you get pregnant?"

"I had a pretty serious bout with anorexia, and it messed up my body. The doctors say there's a chance, but I'm not holding out any hope."

"What about adopting?"

"I know Gregory wants a kid, but only one of his own."

Standing over the sink, Alice splashed some water on her face, reapplied a little make up, and she and Jean returned to the table. Larry had a fresh beer.

"You okay, Babe?" he said solicitously. He looked normal, and with food in him, he had regained some of his earlier self-control, but Alice knew the signs. His voice was a little louder than it needed to be, and his words came a little slower, sounding more like pronouncements than conversation. To someone who didn't know him, he might sound thoughtful. Gregory turned the conversation to the garage and cars.

"You buying any more antique cars, Larry?"

"Still looking. I been sticking close to home, but the best cars are out west. Phoenix or L.A. No snow. No salt. That really eats 'em up" He looked at Alice and smiled.

"There much money in that?"

"Yeah, if you get the right deal. I picked up a '60 Porsche out in Crystal Lake once for five grand, rebuilt the engine, gave it a new coat of paint, and turned it around for eighteen. And I only put two grand into it. Things ain't always that sweet, though."

Alice smiled, and pushed her plate away. Her face felt hot, but her stomach had stopped feeling like it was going to explode. She wondered how many times she had heard the story. It had been the high point of his car-buying, and it was the only one on which he had made so much money. Most of the time, he was lucky to make a few hundred on a car.

As they were finishing, a three piece band started warming up. Larry ordered a round of drinks and another beer for himself. Before the drinks arrived, Gregory leaned over to Larry.

"Mind if I dance with your wife, Larry?"

"I guess it's okay."

Alice stood as Gregory approached her seat.

"Be back in a few minutes," said Gregory.

"You son-of-a-bitch," she said as they walked to the dance floor. "How can you do this and live with yourself? You could be in big trouble if he thinks something's going on."

"From Lar? No, not good old Lar. He doesn't have a clue. Look, I think he's asking Jean to dance."

"Is she a good dancer?"

"She thinks so, but she's terrible. They'll make a nice couple on the floor. She can hold him up. Oh, she must have said no. He's sitting down again."

Gregory pulled Alice as close to him as her belly would allow.

"Are you out of your mind, Greg? You're supposed to be dancing with me out of politeness. I am four months pregnant."

"Yes, I noticed. And with my baby."

Alice tried to wrench her hand from Gregory's grasp, but he held tight. "Once the baby is born, you may want to start working late again."

"That'll be the day. You don't get it, do you? You had your fun, and Larry's got the baby he's always wanted. Everyone wins. Jean and Larry are sitting there watching us." She broke from his grasp and started for the table. "Thanks for the dance, Greg," she said loudly when she was near enough for Larry to hear. "My feet are killing me."

When the music was slow enough, Larry danced with Alice. "Do you have any idea what's going on, Larry?"

"What do you mean?" he asked slowly. "What's going on?"

For a moment, Alice was ready to tell all. That she lived with Gregory in college, got pregnant, and had an abortion. That she had sex with Gregory and was pregnant again. She opened her mouth, but no words came out. Finally, she said, "I think Gregory is laughing at you. A drunk mechanic with dirt under his fingernails. That's what's going on."

"Naw. Greg's my friend. He wouldn't do that. He's my pal."

"I want to go home," she whimpered. "I don't want anything to happen to this baby."

"You mean our son, Jason," he corrected her.

The train ride to Lake Forest went quickly. Larry slept most of the way back. Alice thought about the name. Larry seemed to be stuck on Jason for a boy. Gregory had hinted to Larry that he'd like to be the child's godfather.

When they arrived at the house, Alice asked if they wanted to come in for a cup of coffee before heading back.

"That sounds nice," responded Jean.

Larry stumbled up the walk to the door. "Yeah. You got to see my '65 Mustang. Hey, how about a beer? I can sure use one."

"I think you've had enough, Lar," said Alice. "You've got to get up early, remember?"

Larry stumbled into the kitchen, and they heard the sound of breaking glass. He looked sheepishly through the doorway. "I broke a glass, but it's okay. We got more." Then the refrigerator door thumped and there was a crash of things hitting the floor.

"Maybe we'd better go, Alice," said Jean. We'll take a rain-check on that coffee."

"No, that's okay. Just sit in the living room, and I'll be right there."

"We really better go, Greg." Jean took his arm and led him to the door.

Gregory stopped in the doorway and looked at Alice. "Well, I guess one of these days I'll be Uncle Gregory, right?"

Larry went upstairs. Alice turned out the lights and sat alone in the living room.

CHAPTER 30

▼

After the Auto show, Alice developed a pattern to her life. She went to work, she came home, and she waited for the birth of her child. The days stretched into weeks. Summer turned into fall. Heavy rains caused leaves to remain green until they fell. Only the maples, usually the first to turn red and gold, showed hints of color. Gregory was seldom out of her mind. Her anger and bitterness subsided. There were even moments when she considered herself fortunate. She was going to have a baby. Larry wanted a family and he believed the child was his.

She had committed adultery, and out of that act came the wonderful pregnancy. In her mind floated the thought that her unborn infant would somehow be forced to pay for her mistakes. Her nominal Catholic upbringing, battered by a liberal college education, allowed her to believe there was a force in the universe that balanced evil and good.

The end of January brought a plethora of television programs devoted to birth defects. Larry slept in his chair as Alice felt compelled to watch programs investigating the causes of cerebral palsy, Down's syndrome, and other types of mental retardation.

Jason was born just after midnight on February 19, at Lake Forest Hospital. Larry was sober enough to drive her to the hospital, but in his haste, he took Route 41, and sped right past Deerpath Road.

When Alice learned that Jason had an inguinal hernia, she began crying uncontrollably. She repeated over and over in a barely audible voice, "I knew it! I knew it!"

The staff doctor prescribed a mild sedative.

"It's a common anomaly in infants," the doctor told Larry. "It does require surgical repair, but the operation is pretty routine. Now that you're here, go down to the hematology lab and get yourself blood typed."

"How long will this take? I got work piling up at the garage and I can't afford to spend the day here."

"Not more than fifteen minutes."

Larry walked quickly, following the red lines on the floor to the blood lab. After a short wait, his blood was drawn, and he told the technician to send the results up to his wife."

"Well, we'll have the results in about half an hour. You can come back if you want."

"I can't sit around waiting. I got to get back to work. No work, no money."

"No problem. Just sign this authorization, and we'll send the card up to your wife. What room is she in?"

"I think it's 107B, but I ain't sure."

The lab technician looked at a form in a folder. "Oh, you're having blood drawn because of the surgery on your infant son?"

"Yeah."

"Well, don't worry. Your little guy will be just fine. Doctor Peterson is one of the best pediatric surgeons around."

Later in the afternoon, a nurse came in and handed Alice a small green card with Larry's name and blood type. She looked at the card carefully, tore it into small pieces, and put it into the trash.

A few days after the operation, they took Jason home from the hospital.

"I'm glad he didn't need any blood, Larry. The thought of a blood transfusion into that little arm?"

"Yeah. Good thing. You know, I always thought I was A positive, not B positive. That's what they said when I was in the army. But I guess I'm B positive, just like Jason."

"Well, you know how government paperwork can get fouled up."

"Ain't that the truth. I had a friend who had no middle name, so he put *none* on the form. Guess what his middle name was on his discharge papers. None."

When Larry renewed his driver's license a few months later, he had B positive added on the back for blood type.

"My wife is lucky to have type O," he said to the clerk. "And I got type B positive, same as my son."

CHAPTER 31

▼

Larry wanted to be what he considered a good parent. He limited his drinking to a few beers while he watched TV at night.

One evening Larry walked into Jason's room and stood by the crib next to Alice. "I'm going to build it all for to my son," he whispered to Alice. His beer breath caused her to grimace. "You hear that, Jason? One day everything I have'll be yours." He turned to Alice. "Only thing my old man gave me before he took off was a boot in the ass." He turned back to the bed, his voice a bit louder than before. "I'm going to change the name. McBride's Garage."

Alice walked toward the door of the room. She didn't want him to see the tears.

What'll happen if he ever finds out. He isn't really violent, but any man will lash out if hurt enough.

The baby lay on his stomach, legs spread, head turned to the left to accommodate a thumb. Larry had been surprised by the dark hair, but Alice said it came from her Polish father's side of the family.

"C'mon before you wake him up."

"Yeah, Okay." He felt something rise from his chest to his throat, a message directly from his heart. Pride slipped over him like a diamond necklace, and he smiled at the world.

Larry wanted to show his son the love he never had. His mother had run off when he was five, leaving him to the wrath of his abusive father, Derek, and to the ineffective protection of thirteen-year-old Michael.

Derek would clench his callused, grime-caked hands around Larry's thin arm, dragging him to the hall closet. At first, Larry cried. When he learned that tears were useless, he became silent. Sometimes, Michael would free him, and the two would hide until Derek forgot them or passed out.

When Larry was eight, Derek disappeared, leaving Larry and Michael in the care of a grandmother, who survived on disability and most of the pay from Michael's after-school job.

"Larry," whispered Alice, shaking him from his painful memory. "You wake him and he'll be up half the night," Alice whispered loudly as Larry continued looking into the crib.

"What if he wants to do something else?" Afraid her comment might start an argument, she continued, timidly. "I mean, what if he doesn't want to be a mechanic or own a garage?"

"Then he can sell the business and do whatever the hell he wants. Use the money to go to college. I ain't gonna be one of them fathers who stuffs his business down his kid's throat. Seen 'em come into the garage, telling me their kid's gonna be a doctor or a lawyer like his old man."

Alice nodded agreement. She calculated that Larry would not even be 50 when Jason was ready for college, but she kept quiet, rather than break the mood. Larry wouldn't hear a word she had to say anyway.

CHAPTER 32

▼

The next morning during breakfast, Alice told Larry about the letter she received from her sister. "I guess I'm a little jealous," she said, hoping to entice him into conversation and away from the sports pages.

"Now what?" he looked at her over the paper. "Your sister win the lottery?"

"No. She just took a new job as an account supervisor with Frankel in California. And I'm still working on that damn Cheezie Spread package goods account.

"Shit, California," he said, folding the paper and putting it on the floor while he ate. "Bunch of nuts and faggots. The only thing they got that we ain't is warmer weather and earthquakes."

"Well, it's a real career move for her."

"Yeah, well you got a career upstairs." He finished eating and pushed his chair back, scraping the legs against the floor like fingernails on a blackboard. "Your sister never thought of no one but herself. That's why she's there."

"That's not true. She sent a beautiful gift for Jason."

"Yeah, right. So how come she ain't been in this house since we got married? How come she ain't even seen her only nephew." He looked at his watch. "Hey, I gotta go. Be a little late tonight. Getting together with some of the guys for cards." He put on his jacket and left the house without another word. Alice heard the automatic garage door burr, heard the truck start up, and waited for the door to thud closed.

"Why the hell should Maggie come here?" she said to the wall. "To have more fights with Dad? To be insulted by you?"

The last time she saw her sister was Christmas. Alice was seven months pregnant, and Maggie had flown to Chicago on business.

The two sisters went shopping on Michigan Avenue, and ate lunch at Kaplan's in Watertower, the vertical mall. They reminisced about times they had escaped their parents. Maggie, five years older, had taken Alice on shopping trips for her birthday. Now they were adults, it was even better. They were equals. They talked about jobs and careers and boyfriends and husbands.

We talked about everything except one topic that I never mentioned and Maggie never thought of. When your sister is married and pregnant, you don't usually ask her who's the father.

That morning, after the sitter arrived, Alice walked to the train station. There were still a few patches of the late April snow on the ground. The curb snow was black from exhaust and dirt. The street was chalky white in spots, caked with the residue of the salt. The brisk wind off the lake hit her back and seemed to drive through her heavy coat. The chill awakened her, making her eyes sting.

As she walked by a newspaper vending machine, she saw the headline of The Sun-Times: *Baby Left it to Die in Dumpster.* She bought the paper and read that the baby would lose most of its fingers and toes to frostbite. She couldn't understand how such horror could happen when abortions were legal. She breathed a sigh of relief that she had Jason, and listened to the clackety-clackety-clackety of the wheels.

CHAPTER 33

▼

Eleven months later, Jason took his first unassisted steps. Alice decided to grill steaks in honor of the occasion. She would have suggested wine, but Larry detested wine. He associated wine with alcoholism, and refused to drink any.

As they ate dinner, Larry looked at her and smiled. Jason was in his high chair holding a strip of steak and gumming it vigorously.

"I been thinking, Babe," he said, holding a piece of steak on his fork. His eyes became a deeper shade of blue, and his smile made deep pockets in the corners of his mouth. "You spend a lot of time going to the city to work. What if you had a job where you didn't have to."

"What do you mean?"

"I mean, what if you could work right here. The garage is doing real good. I got people with Jags and Alfas coming in. Shit, I know more about them cars than the people who built 'em."

"So?"

"How bout working for me? You're good with numbers. You could do the billing and set up appointments. Write the checks. Save me from running to answer the phone all the time."

"I don't know, Lar. It's pretty grimy back there."

"I got it all planned out. I'll clean up the area in the back of the shop and make it into a real office. With partitions. All the bathroom needs is a coat of paint and a new toilet."

Alice shook her head. "Lar, I'm just starting to get somewhere again. I lost a lot of ground with the pregnancy. I'm just glad the Cheesie Spread people wanted me back."

"You could even bring Jason. Save having a sitter every day."

"Jason'll need to spend most of his day in a playpen. And holding a crying baby while running a charge card?"

Not only that, I don't want to give up my career to be your gofer.

"In another month they'll owe me two week's vacation, and if I quit, I won't get it."

"So? You wait and take the money. We ain't going nowhere."

"Why not? I thought we were thinking about visiting Maggie. She's always asking us to come out."

"Right. And just leave the garage? Who's going to take care of things? You just saw her when she was in Chicago, didn't you?"

"That was over a year ago. Can't you leave for a few days?" asked Alice. "The guys can handle things. And they can always call you, can't they?"

"And what'll I do from 2,000 miles away? I don't work for someone else. I don't get no paid vacation. If I leave, I gotta pay someone to do my work." He paused. "That's OK. You don't wanna work for me, I can hire someone else."

"Is that so bad?"

"No. Eddie's cousin's looking for a job. You know, the red-head with the big tits."

Alice got up cleared away the breakfast dishes.

"Hope she doesn't get 'em caught in the charge machine." She scraped the dishes hard enough to peel off the design, and clanked them into the dishwasher.

"Hey, I got some cleaning up to do at the shop, and then I'm meeting a guy at Dougan's about buying an old Packard. Why don't you bring Jason and meet me for lunch?"

"He's only a year old. I don't think it's a good idea to take him to a bar for lunch. This's the only day I can get the house cleaned."

"Okay, suit yourself. Be back about five o'clock. Maybe we can go to the movies or something."

"Yeah, sure, if I can get a sitter." After she cleaned, she bundled Jason and took him for a walk in his stroller. The air was cold, but the sky was sunny and clear. She noticed clouds over the lake, but they were not the type to bring snow. When she returned, she started reading a Dean Koontz thriller, *The Bad Place*. She looked at Jason, asleep on the sofa beside her.

This is really working out. I made the right choice. Everything is going to be okay.

At seven, Alice microwaved some leftover meatloaf for dinner. At 8:30, Larry came home.

"So much for the movies."

"Sorry I'm late, babe. That meeting took longer than I thought. We had a couple of beers and a hamburger. Jeez, I'm beat." He got a beer, sat down in his chair, and in ten minutes, he was asleep.

Seething, Alice put on her coat and went for a walk. She couldn't be gone long, because if Jason woke up, Larry'd never hear him. She heard Sarah's voice saying, "If nothing changes, nothing changes."

CHAPTER 34

▼

In addition to hiring Eddie's cousin Rhonda, Larry hired another mechanic. When the garage closed early on Saturdays, Larry would buy his three mechanics and Rhonda a round or two of drinks at The Lamplighter near The Square.

"Just put it on my tab, Al."

"Sure thing, Mr. McBride." Don had been there over a year since Al left. Larry paid his tab monthly, and sometimes added as much as a hundred for a tip, so Don never corrected him.

At dinner, Larry had another surprise for Alice. "I got something in the mail at the shop a couple days ago, about an antique car auction out in Phoenix. If the prices are right, I can make a pile of dough."

"Who's taking care of your work at the shop?"

"The new mechanic's working out good. Besides, I'm only gonna be gone a few days. I worked out a deal with Eddie. He'll take care of things while I'm gone, and I won't fire his cousin."

"She screwing up?"

"Not too bad. A couple times she give customers all the copies, leaving nothing for the records. And I think she got the hots for the new mechanic, who's married. But she's learning. Never worked in a garage before."

"If I can find another cherry like that Porsche, I can make some big money again."

CHAPTER 35

▼

The auction went well. Larry called Alice to tell her he had purchased two vintage Porsches for less than he expected to pay, as well as a couple of other cars, and he was arranging to ship them back to Lake Forest. With rebuilt engines, and a new coat of paint, he could sell them for three times his cost, and cover his plane fare as well.

Big Ed Bartholomew, the auctioneer for Arizona Auto Auctions in Chandler, invited a few high bidders to dinner. Ed was over three hundred pounds, much of which hung over his belt like sacks of potatoes on his six foot five inch frame. His silver hair bounced when he walked.

"Well, you gentlemen have had a successful trip, I'd say."

"I'll drink to that," said Larry. "Let me get the next round. Rosalie, you want a beer or another margarita?" Larry smiled at the petite, dark skinned woman who was Ed's secretary. She smiled back, and the whiteness of her teeth was emphasized in the dim light.

Larry asked Rosalie to dance.

"You're really very attractive, Rosalie." His eyes moved from her face to her breasts, which were pressed against the bottom of his rib cage. He could see the black lace of her bra above the scoop-neck bodice of her blouse.

"Thanks."

He put his arm around her shoulders and leaned on her a bit as they walked back to the table.

"Well," said Ed when they returned, "it's almost eleven, and I've got another big day tomorrow. You need a ride, Rosalie?"

"It's okay," Larry cut in. "I'll see that she gets home safely."

"Don't worry, Ed. I'm a big girl. It'll be okay."

"Then I'll see you tomorrow." Ed put his huge hands on the table and leaned down toward her. "Don't be stupid," he whispered. Then he ambled out toward his truck.

Larry and Rosalie drank a few more beers and margaritas. When they were dancing, Larry kissed Rosalie on the cheek and brushed his hand across her breasts as he spun her. She laughed. When he pulled her close to him, she put her head on his chest and sighed. About 1:00AM, they went back to his motel room.

CHAPTER 36

▼

Two weeks after Larry returned from Phoenix, Alice discovered that Larry's trip involved more than car buying.

"There was a message from Phoenix," Alice said, waiting for his reaction. "Someone named Rosalie wants you to call her."

Larry's head shot up from his newspaper. "She's the secretary of that auctioneer. I asked her to let me know when something good was coming up."

"It didn't sound businesslike. She didn't say anything about cars. Left her home number."

"She's doing it as a favor. Don't want her boss to find out."

"Why would she go to all that trouble for someone she hardly knows?"

Alice walked over to Larry, and with one swipe, ripped the paper from his hands, leaving him holding two small pieces in his hands.

"Maybe I should call Rosalie and find out what she has for you," she shouted, throwing the torn paper onto the floor.

"Are you nuts?" Larry stood up. "What the hell's going on here?"

"That's what I want to know. What's going on?"

"What do you mean?"

"You know damn well what I mean. Don't play dumb with me. Did you fuck her?"

Larry looked at his hands, his fists still gripping the small strips of paper. He pursed his lips, twisting his mouth to one side. His face glowed red.

"Well, answer me, you piece of shit."

Larry looked at the floor. She picked up her book and threw it at him. It struck his head.

Then she stormed into the kitchen, and splashed water on her face, holding the side of the sink to keep from falling to the floor in her anguish. Jason started to cry in his crib upstairs, frightened by the noise.

"You risked my life so you could fuck some Mexican?" she shouted from the kitchen. "How could you do that to me? And to Jason?" she said as she ran up the stairs and picked Jason up, trying to soothe him. Her anger enveloped him, and he cried even harder.

When she returned carrying Jason, Larry put his head in his hands.

"What can I say?" he mumbled into his palms. "It just happened." he muttered. He couldn't look up. He didn't understand why he was smiling, so he didn't raise his head.

"Just happened? That's bullshit. If you want to fuck around, go ahead, but count me out." She walked into the kitchen, banging the door against the wall as she entered. It slowly swung back.

Larry stood and leaned his head against the wall. He hit the wall with his fist, putting a dent in the wallboard. On the second hit, he rammed his fist through, creating a waist-high hole.

For two days, they maintained silence. Larry ate breakfast at the Lake Forest Cafe and dinner at The Lamplighter. On the third evening, Larry turned off the TV and broke the deadlock.

"I don't know why it happened," he said. "I guess the chance was just there and I took it. I never wanted to hurt you."

"You mean you never wanted me to find out. Maybe it's partly my fault. I know my work has sort of taken a chunk of my life. And Jason takes another chunk. That doesn't leave much left."

"What do you wanna do?"

"I need to get away for a while. I've got my vacation time from work. I think I'll go to go to my sister's. She hasn't seen Jason, and, well, I really need to get away from here." She wanted to jump in his lap and tell him she forgave him, but she resisted.

"Yeah, I know what you mean. Maybe that'll be good." He wanted her to stay, to throw her arms around him and kiss him passionately, the way she did before Jason was born. He loved his son, but Jason had altered their lives.

"You do what you need to do," she continued. "Divorce is too easy. That's running away, and I don't want to do that."

"Yeah. Me neither."

"Besides, you couldn't afford it."

His eyes flicked wide open, and he sat up straight.

"But we have to see a counselor. And you need to do something about your drinking."

CHAPTER 37

▼

When Alice returned from California, she started to keep the payroll log for the garage. It stretched her time thin, but she became more involved with Larry. Each Saturday, Alice took Jason to the garage. He slept in a playpen while she went over the records.

Life went on grudgingly for a few weeks. Then, one evening at dinner, Larry pulled a wrinkled, grease stained paper from his shirt pocket. "Eddie said you shorted him his bonus hours last week."

"Well, I used the hours he put on his card."

"Don't you remember what I told you? He does a three hour job in two and a half hours, he gets a bonus half hour."

Alice shook her head and clamped her teeth.

"I'll get Rhonda to log the hours. You can write the checks. Rhonda needs more to do anyway. Maybe she won't have time to pester Miguel. His wife finds out he's fooling around, he's dead meat."

Alice didn't smile. She put the plates of spaghetti on the table and started chopping up noodles for Jason.

The following morning, Alice saw herself full length in the bathroom mirror. She traced a finger over the stretch marks on her breasts, and noted their hollow feel. She placed the palm of her hand on her stomach and pushed. It was no longer flat.

Larry went once to the counselor, and refused to go again. "She's divorced herself for crissake. How the hell's she going to help us? She don't know nothing about nothing."

Alice didn't push it. With a demanding job, a small child and a house, a fight for counseling was an energy check that her body couldn't cash.

CHAPTER 38

▼

Alice awoke, startled by the bang of a door. She thought it was a dream until she heard another thump from downstairs. The digital clock cast an eerie green light in the room. It was three AM. She was alone in bed. Holding the blanket to her chin, she heard more noises. Jason was in the other room. She slid her legs out of the covers, her bare feet touching the cold floor. She silently moved toward the bedroom door. Then the lights flashed on, momentarily blinding her.

Alice squinted in the sudden bright light, throwing her hands in front of her face. "Larry. Oh, shit. It's you."

"Who'd you expect?" He spoke in a slurred exaggerated.

"It's three o'clock in the morning. You trying to give me a heart attack?"

"Scared you, huh?"

"Where the hell have you been? You said you'd be home by 10. I was worried sick."

"Sure you were. You were sound asleep."

"Don't you turn things around, you bastard. Where the hell were you?"

"The time really got away from me, Babe. I kinda got into a card game, and, well, you know." As his voice trailed off, he stumbled into the room and leaned against the dresser, slipping off one untied shoe and dropping it to the floor.

"God damn you! You told me this wouldn't happen again. You promised me." Alice sat on the side of the bed, hugged a pillow across her chest, and leaned forward. You promised me." She started to cry.

Larry looked at her through half closed eyes. He opened his mouth as if to say something, and then he closed it.

She wiped her eyes on the edge of the pillowcase and looked at Larry. The new start she had hoped for after Jason's birth was her delusion. She picked up the shoe. "I want you to get out."

He reached for the shoe with one hand, the other braced against the dresser. She swung it back, holding the toe, and hit him in the chest with the heel. He exhaled loudly, and backed into the wall, the smell of stale beer and cigarettes mixed with the acrid odor of vomit whooshed into the room. Losing his balance, he bumped the dresser, shaking the mirror. Arms raised over his face and head, he sank to the floor.

"Where do you expect me to go? Out in the street?" he whined through crossed arms.

"Go back where you came from," she shouted, throwing the shoe at him. It missed and struck the wall. "There must be another señorita out there desperate enough."

"Never gonna let that go, are ya," he said. When he stood, he held the shoe in both hands, as if he were afraid of it might break.

"Just get out. I really don't care where the hell you go, just get away from me." He turned with exaggerated stiffness and marched toward the door. Jason was crying.

"I'm going to sleep in the camper. You're upset, but you'll feel different in the morning."

"You don't know shit," she said, shouldering past him to the other bedroom.

Taking the one-year old from his bed, she sat in the rocking chair, and hummed to comfort him. When she heard the door to the kitchen close, she went back to bed, taking Jason with her. Six o'clock was only three hours away. She closed her eyes and started to drift into sleep. Jason fell back to sleep, but her eyes wouldn't close.

This time, I'm through. A life without Larry'll be easier. No more wondering where he is or what he's doing. Thinking it might be the police again or the hospital when the phone rings and he's not here. Only Jason to think about.

The sleep of exhaustion caused by anxiety finally captured her. In what seemed like moments, she was awakened by the alarm.

As she picked up Jason and walked into the hall, she heard heavy coughing from the bathroom. She raised her hand to knock, to ask if everything was okay, but changed her mind.

"People don't change," her mother had warned her. "You got to learn to accept, or you'll get broken. When you got expectations, you got disappointments." She had Jason, and a decision to be made.

She yawned as she helped Jason with breakfast. He made a game out of his cereal, as unconscious of the night's events as Larry probably was. Microwaving a cup of yesterday's coffee, she closed her eyes and recalled when she first met Larry.

It was a year after she graduated from college. She was living with her parents in North Chicago. After interviewing for a job in Waukegan, she drove toward the lake to have lunch. When her Ford Fiesta overheated, she pulled in to the Mobil station on Grand and Utica. Larry worked on the car, and joked about it.

When he smiled, his face glowed. His auburn hair seemed to spring from his head in all directions. His freckles grew on top of each other, giving him a clean, country look.

As they got to know each other over the months, he told her of his plan to own a garage. He would work at Mobil for a while, and then get a job with Knause in Lake Forest to learn all he could about expensive foreign cars. She'd been impressed by his ambition.

After they married, they rented a small house in Lake Bluff on Washington Street near Green Bay. Larry worked for Knause for another year, and then took a job as head mechanic at a garage on Green Bay a few blocks from their house. Two years later, he bought the garage. And a year after that, Alice became pregnant for the second time in her life.

CHAPTER 39

▼

Alice put Jason in the living room and went back to her coffee. Larry clumped down the stairs and came into the kitchen.

"You look like you died two days ago." Alice leaned back in her chair and surveyed him. "You sleep in those clothes?"

"No shit." He rubbed his hand over his face and sat down. He coughed, resonant and moist. He went to spit in the sink. "I got to shower and get to work." "Can you believe this shit?" He addressed the ceiling. "I come home late, and I get thrown out of my own house. Got to sleep in a fucking camper on the driveway, for crissake. We got two trani jobs and a motor overhaul hanging up at the shop, and who knows what other shit's coming in. Eddie ain't coming in today, something about taking his mother to the doctor, and I got to sleep in a fucking camper."

Alice looked at him as he carried on.

"What the hell's the matter with you?" His voice trailed off and he looked around the kitchen. "Any coffee?"

"Yesterday's. On the counter." Alice held up her hand to prevent him from continuing his lament or changing the subject. "Do you have any idea what happened last night?"

"I just told you."

"Wrong. I know one thing. I don't want to live like this. Wondering if you've been picked up DUI again. Or worse."

"Well," he said. He stood up and shuffled to the counter. "What do you want me to say? I guess I got a little carried away last night. That a crime?"

Alice was not surprised he didn't remember scaring her or that she hit him with his shoe. "A little carried away? You could hardly stand up. You scared the shit out of me last night. I thought someone broke in."

Larry poured a cup of coffee, heated it in the microwave, and flopped down at the table across from her, holding his cup in both hands. He stared into the dark brown liquid.

"So I got home a little late. Big deal."

"You need to get help."

"It won't happen again. Don't give me that look. I mean it."

"I know you mean it, Larry. But you can't change without help. Maybe you don't really want to."

"What the hell's that supposed to mean? That fucking doctor's full of shit. I don't need nobody telling me I got an alcohol problem."

"Larry, we've gone through this all before."

"Look, I'm telling you, it ain't gonna happen again."

"You said that before."

"What more do you want from me? I swear it ain't gonna happen again."

"How you gonna stop?"

"I just am, that's all."

"Yeah, right. Well, I'm not gonna spend my life in a hopeless situation like my mother. I know what that got her."

Larry sat up and looked surprised.

"Well fuck you. Hopeless, huh. If things are so hopeless, go and file for that goddam divorce. The paper work's all done. But this time there's no turning back. It's for keeps."

That was a phrase her mother used. "It ain't abuse, honey," her mother had said. "That's just the way it is. Marriage is for keeps."

The phrase echoed in Alice's head. *For keeps. For keeps.*

Alice looked up. Larry was standing in the doorway, his arms across his chest. The room darkened as a cloud crossed the face of the sun. Alice could hear the hum of the refrigerator. She always folded in the past. Now, tears burst forth and rolled down her face.

"Well," he shouted. "Now you're gonna find out what it's like to be on your own. I suppose you can always call Gregory. I seen the way you look at him."

She picked up a paper napkin and wiped her face, smudging her cheeks.

"Larry, you're the one who pushed the friendship. I didn't want it. You're so damn impressed by his money."

He walked back to the table and put his face inches from hers. "I'm impressed? And you ain't? Soon's I'm gone you'll probably jump into bed with him. If you haven't already."

"I don't screw my friends, Larry, and I especially don't sneak behind your back."

"How the hell do I know that?" Larry pounded the table with his fist, bouncing Jason's cereal bowl and spilling what was left of the milk.

"Larry, I've done everything I know how to do. Nothing works. I take care of this house. And Jason. I put up with your drinking. And you run around and accuse me of being unfaithful. You're something else."

"One mistake. One fucking mistake, and I'll pay for it the rest of my life."

Alice splashed some water on her face at the sink and wet a cloth to sop up the spilled milk.

"Look," he said apologetically, "if it's money, I can sell a couple of the antique cars at the garage. I know I can get twenty grand for that old La Salle just the way it is."

"Larry, it's not money. It's the way we live. It's the drinking. I don't want to be around when you kill yourself or someone else."

"You make it sound like I drive home drunk every night. There's no pleasing you, is there? I'm still that dumb mechanic who barely finished school, ain't I, you bitch." He raised his arm over her head.

"Larry, don't." Alice cringed.

"Don't worry," he shouted. "I'm out of here. That's what you want, you got it. And I ain't coming back!"

"Larry, you need to get help."

"I'll be moved out by the end of the week. I got friends. I can stay at Eddie's." He walked back up the stairs to the bathroom. "The only thing that'd make you happy is if I dropped dead."

CHAPTER 40

▼

Seven months later, on January 10, Alice left the court as a divorced woman, accompanied by her friend, Sarah Dotson. The sky was washed-out blue, with a few stringy clouds over the lake. The air was cold, even for January, and a biting wind blew powdered snow in waves over the street. Walking down the stone steps to County Street, Alice looked up at the sky and at the statue of the World War One soldier, fifty feet in the air.

"I don't know whether to laugh and be happy or cry and become depressed."

"Quitting isn't a sign of defeat. It's a solution to a problem that could have destroyed you."

Alice had yet to learn that divorce, although easy in detachment, is like losing a finger. The greatest pain comes in healing. She squinted in the sunlight reflected from the snow.

"You really didn't have to come with me, Sarah. But I do appreciate it."

"What are friends for? Anyway, it's a new year, and you have your whole life ahead of you."

"Yeah. I'm going home to an empty house."

"You've got Jason, haven't you. That's hardly empty."

"You're right. I guess I should look on the bright side. You going back to work?"

"Got to. I'll see you tomorrow. Call me if there's anything I can help with."

"Want a ride to the station?"

"Time you get to your car, I'll be there."

As Alice drove past the library, she felt hungry, and remembered Chubby's, a little hamburger place across from the Mobil Station where she first met Larry. As she entered, the smell of a hamburger on the small grill made the juices flow in her mouth. She ordered one from the chunky Korean woman and sat down. There was only one other person in the warm cafe drinking a large coffee, and staring out the window. A homeless woman, wearing several raggy sweaters and an ancient torn jacket. Her lined, dirty face and hands brought tears to Alice's eyes.

She drove home down Sheridan Road through North Chicago past Abbott Labs. Rather than visiting her mother, she decided to keep the day for herself. The trees along Great Lakes Naval Station were skeletons pointing to a sky now turning gray. She thought of driving past everything, but Jason was waiting for her.

Arriving home, she found Jason napping, and Mrs. Garvey stirring a pot of chicken soup on the stove.

"Thought you'd like a some soup to cheer you up, honey. At least, it might make you feel better."

"Thanks, Mrs. Garvey. That's really nice of you."

"Made it at home yesterday, so it's the best today. I'll leave the pot for later. How're you feeling?"

"It's strange. I've been looking forward to this day, and now that it's here, I'm happy I guess, but I sort of regret it. Isn't that odd?"

"Not really. Lots of times we look forward to something so bad that after it happens, we feel a let-down. Things'll get better."

"I hope so."

"You need anything, just call me. I love taking care of little Jason. He's such a dear. He'll talk your ear off. Well, I got to get on home. Got some old ladies like me coming over for dinner."

"Thanks again, Mrs. Garvey. I don't know what I'd do without you."

"You'd find a way. I'll let myself out.

Alice flopped on the sofa and stared at the ceiling, feeling an emptiness rushing in like air filling a vacuum.

She closed her eyes for a few moments, and the sound of the TV woke her. She joined Jason, who was sitting on the floor, and gave him a big hug and a kiss. Putting him on her lap, he started to laugh and she laughed with him.

"Y'know, you're all I really need," she said rocking him back and forth while he laughed harder. "I love you."

"I love you, too, mommy. I'm hungry."

"Just like a man. If you say 'What's for dinner' I'll disown you."

As she walked into the kitchen, the phone rang. Gregory's voice was like fingernails on a chalk board. "Hello, Alice. Figured you'd be back by now. Just wanted to say congratulations and ask if you want some help."

"That's like a Nazi asking a holocaust victim for a date. You're disgusting. If you ever bother me again, I intend to call Jean and tell her everything."

"Okay. Okay. Sorry I bothered you."

She got Jason washed for dinner and sat him in his chair at the table, watching him trying to feed himself chicken soup. The soup ran down his arm as he held the spoon in his fist.

Does Gregory think I'd have anything to do with him now? He's got no power over me any more. He's still trying to control the world.

She took several pieces of chicken out of Jason's bowl and cut them up for him, telling him to use his fork. Watching him put his special cup to his mouth made her realize that he was Gregory's son, which might give Gregory some legal rights.

What if he tries to take Jason away. What if Jean agreed to help him, since she can't have children. No! I've got to put such thoughts out of my mind.

After dinner, she read Jason a story, letting him turn the pages. Then she put him to bed. She walked from room to room, looking at the walls, the pictures, the decorations.

I'm the one who painted all the walls. I'm the one who selected the lithographs. Everything in this house is mine. Not just because we're divorced. They're mine because I selected them and put them in place. Every painting, every book, every ornament, every knickknack. Everything.

CHAPTER 41

▼

After regular visits from the police during the course of a year, the principal at Roosevelt High School asked Bill Forrest to take an unpaid leave of absence until the problem was resloved. The bad publicity, she felt, had impinged on his teaching effectiveness. With the end of the school year less than a month away, he resigned and applied for a newly-opened position at the College of Lake County.

Just after the school year ended, he returned to Roosevelt to pack up his few remaining things, and ran into another English teacher, Susan Forbes, who was cleaning out her desk for the summer.

"Personally, I think you're making a mistake, Bill. You're giving up a $40,000 a year job to go teach in some cornbelt junior college? What'll you do if you're let go after a year? You don't have to resign, you know They can't force you."

She sat on Bill's desk as he squatted to load files into cardboard boxes, his head inches from her ankles. He put his hand on the desk and she placed her hand on his. He could see the bones of her knee outlined through her black nylon running suit At thirty-five and athletic, with straight dark brown hair cut in a page boy, she wore eye make-up and almost no lipstick. Her flirtation with Bill had been department gossip for years.

She leaned toward him. "Whatever happened to innocent until proven guilty?"

"Maybe it's a blessing. Hell, I've been here sixteen years, and I'm teaching the same courses I did in my first year." He put one box on the desk.

"You know I only wish you the best," she whispered, leaning closer to his ear, placing her hand on his. "But I'm really going to miss you. I don't understand how you can take it this calmly. If I were you, I'd be ready to take someone's head off."

"What's the point? Nobody here really gives a shit. Sixteen years and five principals. The new administration doesn't even know me."

Dennis Mayfield, the reading specialist, walked into the room. Susan pulled her hand back from on top of Bill's.

"Well," he said standing and looking at Susan, "at least my paperwork'll be cut. Four classes and a few office hours."

"That beats 6 hours a day of hormonal know-it-alls," she responded, rolling her eyes and looking at the ceiling. "You'll have to let us know how it goes."

He smiled. He would miss her. Four years earlier, the two of them had almost turned the department gossip into a true story.

After chaperoning a school play, Bill and Susan had joined a few other teachers for a drink at a local bar. One by one, the others had left. They decided to have another drink and then dance. He had enjoyed holding her close and she hadn't resisted, the drinks loosening his normal reserve. When the music stopped and they sat down, they were both silent for a minute, looking at each other.

"You're an attractive man, Bill," Susan said, taking his hand. "And we're not doing anything wrong."

"I think we'd better leave," he responded, not letting go of her hand. When they stood up, he helped her with her jacket, putting his arm around her shoulders as they walked to the parking lot. "You're right," he said. "Nothing wrong with a couple of colleagues having a drink, is there?"

"Not at all. Nothing wrong with it at all."

As she stepped up into Bill's Pathfinder, her short skirt slid up to her thighs. As soon as Bill got into the car, she grabbed the lapels of his coat, pulled him toward her and kissed him hard. Leaning toward her, his hand started at her knee and slid higher. Her thigh felt warm to his touch. He stopped when he felt the hem of her bikini panties. She loosened her grip, sat back, she laughed softly, and pulled down her skirt. He sat up and started the engine.

"Where to?" he asked.

"I don't know. I've never done this before. Do you live close by?"

"No. It's almost an hour to my place. You?"

"Closer." She paused. "But Grant's home." She laughed. "You suppose he'd think it odd if I don't come home tonight?" She laughed again and then stopped abruptly, tears in her eyes.

He reached over and hugged her as she put her head on his shoulder. "You know something, Susan. It's probably better this way. We'll be able to look at each other and smile tomorrow." He never knew if her tears were caused by sadness, embarrassment, or relief.

CHAPTER 42

▼

Bill left the high school, headed toward the outer drive and turned north. The parks and the deep green of the trees outlined against the blue sky and white clouds, distracted him. Exiting at Hollywood, he followed Sheridan and crossed Morse Avenue.

What a terrible name for a street. Glad I'm getting out of here. Too bad I'm not moving to another state, rather than closer to where that bastard Morse died.

For ten years he had lived in the same apartment on North Sheridan Road overlooking Lake Michigan. The memories of Marissa and Andrew were imbedded in the walls. He wondered if the next tenants would know. Now, all his material possessions were packed, waiting for him in a few boxes. He had sold his furniture, given away his old television set, and kept just what he absolutely needed. Moving was a way to pare down to simplicity.

Driving by a police car on North Sheridan, he imagined their eyes following him. He smiled.

"If they're waiting for me to tell someone, it'll never happen. That son-of-a bitch got what he deserved," he said aloud, talking to an imaginary passenger.

"Well, it was premeditated killing. But you're right. He didn't deserve to live. Remember what Dad always said. Never Again."

"Yeah. I remember."

It was a phrase his father had used many times. Never allow anyone to hurt you or your family with impunity. Bill had an image of his father, dressed in his business suit, speaking with his clipped British accented English. He also remembered his father's one run-in with the Chicago police.

CHAPTER 43

▼

George Forrest was not a particularly big man, nor was he violent. Just five feet seven, he and his gaunt wife Rebecca emigrated to the United States from Austria a half-step ahead of the Nazis. He had learned English from British schoolteachers, who helped him get a passport to Canada. When he entered the United States, he legally changed his name from Isaac Baumgarten, and stopped believing in a God who could allow the Holocaust to happen.

A man in the local neighborhood grocery store, unaware of George's Jewish background, complained loudly that the Jews were responsible for most of the world's problems, and had caused all the suffering in Europe. George told the man he was crazy, and anyone who would listen to him was also crazy. When George turned to leave, the man knocked him down and swore at him. When George stood, the man punched him, bloodying his nose.

George ran from the store and returned moments later with a baseball bat. With one swing, he broke the man's arm. George spent a night in jail, but no complaint was ever filed.

In the car, Bill nodded his head in assent. "Yeah. Never again."

CHAPTER 44

▼

After he accepted the teaching position at the College of Lake County, Bill called his friend George Dotson in Lake Forest. They had known each other since college. George took him to lunch at Washington Square in Highwood, to congratulate him.

"I'm looking forward to teaching up here, George," he said between bites of his favorite meal of angel-hair pasta with garlic and olive oil. "Tell Sarah I'll be happy to come by for dinner several times a week."

George had laughed, "I'd be happy just to have her just cook dinner several times a week. Time she gets home from work she's too tired to do anything."

"She still working downtown? I thought she was going to quit."

"Worse. Now she's decided to drive in every day."

"In all that traffic?"

"You figure it. Says she enjoys the solitude and listening to books on tape. Me, I'd be so frustrated I'd go crazy. I can understand road rage."

As they had coffee, George saw an opportunity. "Well, professor, you need to buy a house."

"You're not going to start that again. I don't want a house."

"Quite a few nice ones for sale in Grayslake. Good investment, and you can use the tax write-off."

"Spoken like a true real estate salesman. I hate the thought of caring for a house. I hate yard work. I hate cutting grass. And I hate shoveling snow."

"Not to worry, my friend. Plenty of townhouses. You keeping your place in the city?"

"Nope. I'm going to get a place in a motel in Grayslake for a few weeks. Then I'm heading to Wyoming to camp for a month."

"A motel? That's crazy Why don't you stay with me and Sarah until you get yourself settled. We'd love to have you. The house is pretty quiet since Janet got married."

A few days after that lunch, Sarah had called to confirm George's invitation. So it had been decided. He would stay with them until he could find a place of his own.

Now, as he drove north on Skokie Highway toward Lake Forest in the early evening, he was forced to stop for an accident at Clavey Road. The spinning red light of the ambulance and the flashing white and blue lights of the police cars gave the scene a surreal, dream-like effect. He imagined the face of Robert Morse, first smiling at the trial, and then flattened against his windshield. Shaking his head vigorously, he muttered, "You got just what you deserve. I only hope you knew it was me."

After a few moments, a policeman motioned him through. He kept his eyes straight ahead, anxious to see George and Sarah.

CHAPTER 45

▼

Lying in bed in the spare bedroom one evening when George and Sarah had gone out, Bill turned on the TV and flipped to the news.

"In local news, a small plane went down into Lake Michigan after taking off from Waukegan Airport. The pilot and three passengers, a man, his wife and small son, all from Springfield, were killed."

Tears glazed his eyes. He felt a pain in his abdomen, empathy with the family.

He changed channels. The noise of the TV faded away as he closed his eyes.

As he had done many times, he saw a woman and a boy frozen in a crosswalk. A car doesn't stop as it makes a left turn. The car slams into them. They fly in slow motion. He runs toward them. But he always arrives too late. They both sit up and point at him.

The next morning at breakfast, Sarah poured coffee. "You're not planning on going anywhere, are you, Bill? You'll be around for my party."

"What party?"

"Sarah decided it'd be nice to have a party on the—what's it called—you know, the first day of summer."

"Solstice. It's called the solstice." Sarah reached for a piece of toast. "I thought it'd be a nice way to kick off the summer, and have a few friends in." She looked at George, brushed some crumbs into her hand and deposited them on a plate.

"Wait a minute. You trying to fix me up again?"

"I told you, Sarah," said George, smiling at Bill. "Things have to take their own time."

"Well, I think it is time. You've had enough alone time Bill. Now it's time to be with people. You're not getting any younger. I just think it's time." Her voice increased slightly in volume.

"No sense arguing with you when your mind is made up. June twenty-first, huh. I'll be around."

"Actually, I'm planning it for June twenty-second. The twenty-first is a Friday, and I need a day to get everything ready."

"So who've you lined up for me? I want a brunette, about five feet seven or eight, a hundred five to a hundred fifteen pounds, between twenty-eight and thirty-five. How's that?"

"Anything else. What about money. You want her to be rich?" asked George.

"Well, she ought to have a good job. And be a college graduate, BA at least."

"So far, you've described a good friend of mine. I think I'll invite her to the party."

"Like you weren't planning to," said George.

CHAPTER 46

▼

Gregory called at work again.

"Why don't we have lunch today," he said, sounding as if he were inviting someone to a business meeting.

"I told you yesterday we have nothing to discuss."

"Don't hang up. This will be strictly business. We need to discuss your new job."

"What the hell are you talking about?" She slammed the phone down on its cradle.

She knew what he was talking about. The rumor was that Cheesie Spread was looking for a new agency. That would leave Alice with no major account, and possibly no job. No job meant no money for house payments, and she knew she couldn't count on Larry. She felt the acid rise in her throat, and tasted the vomit.

A job with Varonian and Varonian. But Gregory's not above playing mind games. What else does he want?

She stared out the window at the haze over the city. The sky was obscured today, and the noise of traffic reached her in muted honks and roars.

She called Gregory back and agreed to meet him for lunch in a very public place. He told her he had no problem with that. "We have nothing to hide, do we?"

"You're right. Nothing to hide." *Nothing except a two-year-old child.*

"I can't make it until later today. A problem has come up with a new account. I'd like to talk to you about it, though. How about three-thirty."

Alice took the offensive. "Look, if this is another one of your jokes, I don't find it funny. And I want to meet in a very public place."

"I can't talk right now. I'm supposed to be in a meeting that started five minutes ago. How about meeting me at three o'clock at the Pizza Due? That public enough?"

When Alice arrived, she found Gregory and the pizza was waiting.

"Deep dish vegetarian, just the way you like it. I told you I had to talk to you. And I figured the pizza would add a nice touch. We've talked over pizza before. You want a beer?"

"I'll have a diet soda. I've stopped drinking."

"I can understand that. How is Larry. I haven't seen him for a while."

"You ought to call him. You're his friend. You can still look him in the eye, can't you?"

"Yeah, I probably should call, but you know how it is. I guess I could go by the garage at least."

"I just had a thought. What if Jean came walking by?"

"She can't. She's up in Green Bay at some kind of retreat."

"Oh."

The taste of the pizza reminded her of the last one they had shared. The day before he went to Chicago, they had made love and had eaten pizza in bed watching a movie on television. In her mind, she could see herself, covers pulled up to her armpits, leaning against the wall in the small bedroom. She could feel the warmth of their bodies touching, and smell the olives and green pepper.

She put the slice back onto her plate. "This is nuts. What's the deal on this job?"

"It's still only a possibility. I may be going after a package goods account with Manischewitz."

"The wine? Don't they make that awful sweet wine?"

"They make lots of things. One is matzos for Jewish Passover. Another is snack crackers. I'd like to sell them on the strength that they could increase their share of the snack cracker market."

"That's it? That's what this is all about? Snack crackers?"

"There's more. I'm pitching Cheesie Spread, and if they decide to come with us, that's where you come in. They'll be more likely to come on board if I tell them you're coming, too. They like your work. It seems I may need you, and I'll make it worth your while. If you stay at HCB, you may not have a job."

Don't I know that. I'd have to scramble, and take the first thing that comes along, like it or not.

"That's something I need to think about," she lied. She had already decided to take Gregory's offer, but she didn't want to seem too anxious. "But, I want you to know something, Greg. I won't put up with any crap from you. I'll go to Jean if I have to. Nishan and Schwartz, too. You mess with me and I'll take you down so hard they'll suck you up with an eye dropper."

CHAPTER 47

▼

The evening of Saturday, June 22, Alice stood outside the home of Sarah and George Dotson, wondering whether to knock or run away. It had been impossible to say no to Sarah.

Alice was in no mood to meet people. She arrived late, planned to stay for an hour to be polite, and then leave. That was an effective compromise. She would please everyone.

She listened to muffled sounds of laughter and music for a moment, and then rang the bell. Alice fluffed her hair and stepped back when the door burst open.

"I'm so glad you came," gushed Sarah as she greeted Alice at the door, throwing her arms around the younger woman. With her mouth close to Alice's ear, she whispered, "There's someone I really want you to meet."

"Oh, no, Sarah, you didn't."

"Didn't what?"

"You know what I mean. Invite someone here for me."

"No, I didn't invite someone here for you," Sarah smiled. "He happens to be living here. For the summer."

Sarah took her by the hand and almost dragged her the few feet to the hall closet.

"You can't imagine how nervous I am," Alice said, as she slipped off her jacket. She looked at her arms, imagining the gooseflesh would be obvious to everyone. "I haven't been out since Larry left."

"What's it been, four, five months?"

"Six."

"Well, just have a drink and relax. And remember. We're your friends."

She took Alice's hand again and led her down the hall to the French doors that opened into the living room. Alice's once permed light brown hair now hung straight and flowed to her shoulders, accentuating her dark eyes. She hoped to recapture the athletic look of her college days. Her forest-green, scoop-neck silk blouse and dress shorts shimmered as she moved.

About ten people were seated on chairs and the sofa around a light wood coffee table facing a fireplace. The far wall had large windows and a door that opened to an enclosed wooden deck.

"For those who don't know her," Sarah raised her voice as if she were giving a speech. "This is Alice Solinsky. You'll have to introduce yourselves later."

Just as she passed the doorway, Alice heard a familiar voice.

"Hey, Alice, c'mon and join us." Jean Varonian was just walking in from the deck outside. "We haven't seen you for ages."

Alice was stunned. It had never occurred to her that Sarah might invite Jean and Gregory.

"Hold on," said Sarah. "She'll be right back." She poured a glass of red wine from the decanter on a table just inside the French doors, and took it to Alice, who had walked a few feet down the hall.

"C'mon. I want you to meet Bill. I've told him about you, and he's dying to meet you."

"What did you tell him?"

"Only that you were divorced and you were coming to the party."

"Sarah, I don't want to meet anyone."

"He's a college English teacher and loves to travel. What an interesting man. If I didn't have George, I'd go after him myself."

Alice recalled her college English teachers.

What could be stuffier? Sarah described him as interesting, which meant fat and homely.

Alice pulled back. She felt the same way when she was twelve and her mother's high school friend had come to town with her son. Alice had to go to a movie with fourteen-year-old Jeffrey. The two were told they had played together as infants. Now, they were both trapped in the fantasy of their mothers.

"Sarah, you don't know how I feel." She crossed her arms to protect herself. A volcano grumbled in her stomach. "I'm alone because that's what I want right now. I was alone when I was married to Larry but I didn't know it. This is better.

"There's no pressure, Alice. He's just a nice guy, and heaven knows, you need to meet a nice guy."

"What'll I say?" Her shoulders slumped.

"Don't worry. He isn't going to ask you to marry him. If he asks you out to dinner or something, you can always say no. What've you got to lose?"

Sarah opened the door, and Alice took the fatal leap into the kitchen. She saw Bill standing at the far end of the room, a little taller than the refrigerator he leaned against. His thinning, wispy brown hair reached to the base of his neck, and seemed to be flying into his glass of beer as he took a sip. The sleeves of his navy blue sweater were pushed up, displaying muscular arms. His feet were crossed, and he had slipped off one of his brown loafers, exposing a small hole at the heel of his tan sock. He was talking to George.

Bill turned as Alice entered the room. He stopped talking and quickly slid his foot into his shoe. Their eyes were momentarily tied by an almost visible thread.

"Well, Bill," said George. "I think you've found someone more interesting to talk to than me."

Before Sarah had a chance to introduce them, Bill moved toward Alice. "You must be Alice. Hello. I'm Bill Forrest. Sarah mentioned you might come."

"I'm happy to meet you, Bill. I'm Alice Solinsky." She extended her hand, and Bill took it in both of his, not letting go for several seconds longer than seemed normal, but Alice didn't think to withdraw it.

Sarah turned to George. "Let's get the rest of the cold cuts and take them into the living room."

"Good idea, Sarah. Now, don't get carried away, you two. We'll be right back."

Both Bill and Alice laughed nervously.

Bill motioned Alice toward a chair at the small oak table and then sat down across from her. "It really is nice to meet you, y' know. Sarah has told me a little about your recent divorce, and I can imagine what you're going through."

"I don't think there's anyone she hasn't told. You divorced?"

"It's a long story."

He told how his wife and son had been killed by a drunk driver, and he had gone into a year-long depression. Alice could see the pain in his eyes when he spoke about Andrew.

Bill loves the son who was taken from him. Gregory has a son he'll never acknowledge. And Larry loves a child he thinks is his.

Alice found herself opening up about her relationship with Larry, the womanizing, the drinking. The unburdening made her feel light.

"Would you like a beer?"

"No, thanks. I've still got my wine. I guess after the problems I've gone through with my ex, I'm not much of a drinker."

Alice talked about her job with Cheesie Spread, and Bill told her about his teaching at the high school and his new position teaching at the College of Lake County. She had not felt this happy and relaxed for a long time.

CHAPTER 48

▼

The kitchen door opened. When Alice saw who it was, the smile dropped from her face with a thud, and she jumped up, knocking her chair back into the wall. The hair on the back of her neck crinkled, and she gripped the table for support.

"Hi, Alice," Gregory said. "George said you were back here. Am I interrupting something?"

A flood of anger raced through her. They had spoken only twice since the divorce. Once when Gregory had called to offer what he called his sympathy, and when he suggested she might work for him.

"No, we were just talking," Bill said, introducing himself.

Alice mumbled, "Where's Jean?"

"She's in the other room, talking to Sarah."

Alice excused herself, and found Sarah in the dining room.

"What's the matter, Alice?"

"Nothing. Except Gregory Varonian. "He offered me a job with his agency, and I don't know if I want to work for him. He's still friends with Larry, and that complicates things."

"Oh. Maybe it's a chance for more money. God knows, you could use it."

"And there's the other problem." Alice looked at the floor and her face flushed cranberry.

"What do you mean?"

"I don't know what to do about Cheesie Spread. I think they're looking for another agency."

"That's the rumor. Is Gregory trying to land the account?"

"I don't know. Sarah, I'm sorry. I really have to leave."

As she put on her jacket, both Bill and Gregory walked out of the kitchen. Bill smiled at her. Gregory stopped.

"Can I talk to you in the kitchen for a minute, Alice?"

"Is it about the new job?" burst in Sarah. "Alice doesn't have many secrets from me."

"Well, yes, it is, as a matter of fact." He took Alice's arm and pulled her into the hall, speaking quietly. "I really want to talk to you."

"Yeah, but not here. If you're really serious about the job, I'll call you at your office Monday."

At that moment, George burst into the room shouting. "Hey, everybody," We're going to play a game. Everyone pick a partner. Bill started to move toward Alice, but Gregory took her arm and led her to one side.

"I guess we could be partners again. What do you think?" he said smiling.

Alice pulled her arm away and growled, "I think you better partner with your wife."

George began explaining the rules of the new game he had devised.

"Oh, no, George," said someone sitting on a chair in the corner. "Not another one of your famous games. Count me out. After the last so-called game, I thought I was going to have to sleep out with the dog." Several people laughed and argued the merits of the previous game.

Alice looked at her watch. "Oh my God. Mrs. Garvey said she wanted to leave by eleven, and I promised I'd be back by then. She has friends coming over tomorrow, so she wanted to get home early. Thanks for inviting me, Sarah. Sorry. I'll see you Monday."

As Sarah helped her on with her jacket and the two women walked toward the door, Bill approached Alice. "Wish you didn't have to rush off so soon."

"I promised the sitter I'd be back by eleven. Here's my phone number. Call me."

"Sure," Bill said. As Alice left, he stood there, looked for a moment at the small piece of paper, folded it in half and slipped it into his shirt pocket. Babysitters. He had almost forgotten that problem.

He sat down on the sofa and listened to George, who was pretending amazement that his suggestion for a game had been rebuffed.

CHAPTER 49

▼

The drive for Alice was short, and spinning thoughts made it even shorter.

Bill seemed really interesting. And he's good looking. Damn, I'm just not ready.

And the thought of working for Gregory. But if he offers me enough money? I can always quit. I managed to survive the line at Abbott, so I can put up with almost anything.

Pulling up in her driveway, she turned the engine off, leaving the car outside. She had a hard time putting the key in the lock. The porch light was out again.

"Hi, mommy." David Letterman threw a card and Jason laughed at the sound of breaking glass. Jason was wearing one of Larry's old tee shirts. It was so large that only his feet and hands could be seen. The Lion King pajamas he cried to have were in the drawer.

"Why are you still up? It's eleven o'clock."

"Every time I put him to bed, he'd get up and run down stairs," said Mrs. Garvey.

"Oh, Mommy," Jason said with mock adult tone, "Tomorrow is Sunday and we can sleep late." He drooped his head and shoulders as he spoke, allowing his unruly dark hair to hang forward.

Alice opened her purse and took out her wallet.

"Don't be silly, Alice. I enjoy looking after little ones. Keeps me young."

"Thanks, Mrs. Garvey. If there's anything I can do for you, let me know."

The older woman left as Jason ran to the kitchen, and came back with a bent piece of red art-board in his hand made to look like a large greeting card. "Look what I made for you today, Mommy." He held his creation over his head.

"What is it?"

"It's a card. I made it for you. Mrs. Garvey helped me." In large shaky, wobbly letters, the words "FOR MOMMY" danced across the top. Underneath the letters was a scene that looked like sticks with balls on top, colored in blue, green, yellow, brown and orange.

"That's beautiful, Jason. Thank you."

"That's the mommy, and that's the daddy, and that's me."

Alice started to cry. She picked him up, gave him a hug and a kiss, and held him tightly. She thought of Mrs. Garvey, old and living alone, existing on memories along with morning coffee.

"And now young man, it's up to bed right now. I don't care that tomorrow's Sunday. I don't want a crabby kid on my hands all day."

As Jason started slowly up the stairs, the phone rang. Alice picked it up and recognized Gregory's voice.

"What the hell do you want? I told you I'd call you Monday at your office."

"I need to firm up the job offer."

"I'm just putting Jason to bed. Mrs. Garvey let him stay up to wait for me." She yelled up the stairs. "Get into bed, Jason. I'll be there in a minute."

"Do you think he'll ever know?" Gregory asked.

"He'll know when you tell him. When you tell everyone and take responsibility for your son! Greg, I don't need this shit on top of everything else. Is this what'll come with the job?"

"Call me tomorrow."

A wave of exhaustion washed over Alice. She was suddenly too tired to argue. "I'm really beat. I'm going to bed."

"Call my home office in the morning. We can meet for lunch at Art's Old House."

"Okay, okay." He had won again.

Alice trudged up the stairs to Jason's room. When she looked in, he was asleep. Her head was pounding, and she knew she had to take some aspirin, but she lay down on her bed and began to cry. At first she cried silently, but then her sobs caused her to shudder. She didn't want to wake Jason, so she turned over and muffled her cries in a pillow sham. She thought she might vomit as she fought to get her breath. After a few minutes, her sobbing eased. Still crying silently, she started to get undressed, kicking off her shoes and slipping off her skirt, leaving them where they fell. She stood there in her blouse and panties, looking at her face in the full length mirror, watching the black tears running down her cheeks. As she reached for a tissue, the phone rang again, startling her.

"Now what does he want? It's almost midnight."

"Hello?" Sitting on the side of the bed, her voice sounded weak and far away.

"Hello, Alice. It's Bill. You know, from the Dotson's party?"

"Yes, of course. Bill." She lay down and smiled.

"I hope I'm not disturbing you."

"No, no. I was just getting ready for bed."

"The party is just breaking up. Is everything OK?"

"Yeah. Fine. Thanks for calling."

"Well, there's another thing I want to ask. I know it's awfully late. I'm glad you're still up. Would you like to go to brunch tomorrow? Maybe we can take in the art festival in Old Town afterwards. We didn't really have much time to talk, and this'll give us a chance to get to know each other a little."

"I don't know, Bill."

"We could meet somewhere if you want. No pressure. Jason might enjoy it, too."

"Well…"

"There's a nice place called Egg Harbor behind The Square. You know it?"

"Yes."

"I'll meet you there at nine. I won't take no for an answer. Just say yes."

"Okay. But how about ten thirty."

"Great. See you then. G'night." He hung up quickly.

Gregory's after me for something, probably more than the job. Bill seems too good to be true. And tomorrow I'm going to see them both.

She finished undressing, wiped her face with a warm washcloth, and lay in bed, her eyes closed. The cool, soon-to-be-warm weight of a blanket caressed her skin, its weight reassuring her body. She rolled to her stomach, pulling the sheet and quilt up over her shoulders, the side of her face buried in the pillow.

Be careful, be careful, be careful. The sound of her inner voice reverberated through her head.

CHAPTER 50

▼

Alice woke at seven with a headache that made her want to take four extra-strength aspirins and sit in a dark room. Bright light was painful.

She felt a hurricane forming. It could destroy her and Jason. Hearing Sesame Street on the TV downstairs, she considered going back to sleep. Jason could put cereal in a bowl and pour milk into it when he was hungry. But it was be easier to make breakfast than to clean spilled milk and Cheerios from the carpet.

Brunch with Bill at 10:30 and then lunch with Gregory. Why the hell did I do that? Damn!

There was coffee left from the previous day. Half a cup of mud. She used it to wash down three aspirins, and then called Jason to the table.

"Can I eat by the TV, Mommy?"

"OK, but try not to spill."

"I won't." He took his bowl of cereal and almost tripped on the throw rug as he trotted into the living room.

Why don't children ever walk. Always in a hurry to get somewhere, but they don't know where and they don't know why.

Gregory dangled the prospect of the job, but there was a big hook. The only reason she'd considered it was a better salary. She could always sell the house and quit. Two realtors told her people were interested in her area. With her equity, she could cash out a small two bedroom condo closer to the city.

Alice lay on the sofa. Thoughts of Bill and Gregory popped up behind her closed eyes like targets in a shooting gallery. Each time she shot one, the other jumped up.

What are Bill's problems. He seems nice, but no one's problem free. Sarah knows him, and I trust Sarah.

Gregory. I was a willing accomplice in my own seduction. I should tell him to drop dead.

"He'll have to pay me a damn good salary," she said to Jason, who was still in front of the TV. "Working for the esteemed firm of Varonian and Varonian after all these years. What a joke. I couldn't get a job there when I needed one. I guess Grandma was right. It just takes patience." She looked at her son, engrossed in the latest episode of Cookie Monster, and shook her head.

The pain in her head was finally reduced to a twinge. She made a fresh pot of coffee and continued her monologue with Jason. "Talk about irony. Jean's the one who suggested the job in the first place." Alice looked at the clock again. "Eight. It's too early to call Gregory, I don't know Bill's number."

She thought again about the party the evening before.

"Hey, he's staying with Sarah and George." She dialed their number, and Sarah answered.

"Alice, what're you calling so early for? It's barely eight o'clock."

"I wanted to speak to Bill. Is he up? We're supposed to have brunch later." She could almost see Sarah smiling, and heard the muffled sounds of Sarah waking George. After a few minutes, Bill answered.

"Hi, Alice." He sounded cheerful, even this early in the morning. "I hope you're not calling to break our date."

"No. But I promised to take Jason over to a my mother's this afternoon. You know what Grandmothers are like," she lied. There was silence. She wanted to take her words back as soon as she said them. She hated using Jason for her lie, but she had no choice. "Can we make the brunch a breakfast?"

"Well, sure, that's no problem. They don't take reservations anyway, so we may have to wait a bit. How about 9:30?"

"Could we make it 9:00? I need to get back so Jason can get cleaned up before we go."

"Sure, no problem."

"Meet you there. And that way we'll have a little more time," she added as an afterthought, hoping to soften the sharpness of the abrupt change.

Lying made her feel vulnerable. As a child, she imagined the ability to know lies came with being a parent. Would she be able to tell with Jason? She took a quick shower and put on a striped oxford shirt and jeans.

Jason was still watching TV when she came downstairs. He complained. "I don't want to go. I want to watch TV." He folded his arms and refused to move.

"I thought you liked eating at the restaurant. They've got all kinds of nice things. Eggs and pancakes. Even French toast."

"I'm not hungry."

"We don't have much time." She took his hand. "Now let's wash your hands and face and let's get dressed."

CHAPTER 51

▼

As she parked her car, Alice saw Bill at an outside table. It was ten minutes after nine. She picked Jason up and carried him across the street.

"Got lucky," he said. "Looks like we won't have to wait after all."

Jason kneeled on a chair and stared at the table.

"Well, you must be Jason." Jason continued to look at the table.

"Jason, say hello. He's a bit shy the first time he meets anyone."

"Hell-low," said Jason to the table. He reached his hand in Bill's direction spilling a glass of water. Bill was quick enough to escape the waterfall, which soaked his chair. Bill tried unsuccessfully to get into a conversation with Jason. Finally, he just shrugged and smiled at Alice.

To appease Jason, Alice ordered chocolate milk and French Toast to share with him. When the milk came, Jason pushed the glass away. It rocked and came dangerously close to spilling again. Bill quickly steadied it.

"When you have little kids, you seldom get to eat what you really want in a restaurant," Bill said trying to sympathize.

After breakfast, he picked Jason up and took Alice's hand. "I'd like to see you again," he said as they walked toward her car.

"I'd like that, too, Bill. Next time, he stays home. That way we might be able to talk to each other."

"I'm pretty well swamped this week with preparation for my new classes and finding a place of my own, but how about next Saturday night. We could have dinner and take in the new French film at the Fine Arts."

"That sounds great. The last time I spoke a word of French was in high school. Call me during the week, and we'll make plans."

Alice put Jason in his car seat and then turned to Bill. "I guess you don't usually have to put up with a cranky child on the first date."

"I think it's a first." He turned to Jason. "Bye Jason. Maybe next time we'll have more to talk about."

Jason pursed his lips, puffed up his cheeks, stared straight ahead, and said nothing.

"Well, Jason, that's the end of that. What a disaster. Spilled water, syrup all over the table and your face, and almost the entire time spent coaxing you to say something. Now I have to get ready for lunch with Gregory. Every time I've had anything to do with him it's ended in disaster. Maybe I shouldn't get involved with him again. What do you think?"

Jason, just about to fall asleep in his car seat, nodded his head as if in response.

CHAPTER 52

▼

She lay Jason on the sofa and called Gregory. They agreed to meet at two o'clock. She changed her clothes, and called Mrs. Garvey, who agreed to give Jason lunch when he woke up.

The drive to Rondout was quiet. When traffic was stopped by a freight train on Route 176, it didn't bother her. She welcomed the extra time to think.

In the parking lot, people were getting out of another car. She imagined them talking about her as she climbed the sagging stairs, opened the old wooden door, and walked in. Gregory was nowhere to be seen.

At 2:20, Greg walked in, looked around, saw her, and walked to the bar.

"Hi, Mr. Varonian," boomed the bartender. "You want a drink?"

"Yeah, Tony. I'll have a whiskey and water. Make it a double."

Tony chatted with Greg as the drink was made, and then Greg walked slowly to the table. He came here often enough to be known by name, but that was his style.

"Still late, Greg. Some things never change."

"It's only 20 minutes. I got tied up on the phone. That KFC account'll take some doing. You could do it in a heartbeat. Just flash a sexy smile and let them know that there are brains behind it, and they'll eat out of your whatever. You know the drill."

"You wouldn't let me near the KFC account for anything and you know it."

"Don't say 'for anything.' I might take you up on it."

She looked at the menu. The thought of more food now almost made her gag.

"I take it by your tenseness that you're interested in the job?"

"I don't know about that," she said flippantly. "I can only tell you after I hear the salary."

"Well, I'll be honest with you."

"Really? That'll be a first."

"When it comes to business, I don't screw around. If you really want the job, there's an opening. Manischewitz contacted me about their snack cracker line, and I could use someone with your background. And the Cheezie Spread people are impressed with you."

"You mean they'll come over if I do? What kind of money are we talking?" Alice sat up straighter in her chair. This was her leverage. He might be a rat in his personal life, but he knew the business. In six years he had taken Varonian from a small shop to an operation with its own creative and graphics department.

"Well, I know what you're making at HCB I'll up it $10,000 a year with a $10,000 sign-on bonus. If things go well, there'll be yearly bonuses as well."

Alice remained calm. She had expected less. She had nothing to lose. He had made the offer. "Oh, I had hoped for more than that. I'm being reviewed for a management position at HCB. Besides, I thought I would be—what did you call it—an asset."

"Cut the crap, Alice. Once they lose Cheesie Spread, there'll be nothing for you to manage. You know what this business is like. I can go 15 and 15 and that's the limit. But you'd better produce."

Alice smiled. *Gregory trying to fire me. Once I'm in, it'll be 'till death do us part. I won't leave until I'm good and ready.*

Gregory ordered a hamburger with fries, sliding the fries onto a separate plate so Alice could eat them. He wanted her to give notice to HCB immediately and start in three weeks. She was elated with the salary. But her joy had a dark edge.

"Remember, Greg. This is a job, nothing more."

"Yeah, right. A job."

CHAPTER 53

▼

After she gave notice at HCB, Alice had days filled with anxiety. She talked to Sarah every day about the move.

When Bill called to confirm their date for Saturday night, she almost had to ask who he was. In all the tumult of her life, she had almost forgotten about him. But that was about to change.

CHAPTER 54

▼

Michael called. "Hi Alice. I need to come by. It's important that I talk to you, and I can't do it from here on the phone."

"Sure, Mike."

"Great. See you in half an hour."

Alice sensed the urgency in his voice, making her think something had happened to Larry. It wasn't like Michael to be cryptic.

She recalled the night Larry ran his truck into a center divider on Skokie Highway. Michael took her to visit him at Saint Therese Hospital, where they were assured that Larry's mild concussion was not as life-threatening as his drinking.

Alice wished that Larry was more like Michael. Yet it was the weakness, the tough little-boy-lost quality that had caused her to fall in love with Larry in the first place.

When Michael knocked, she was waiting for him. Instead of hello, she blurted, "Michael, what's wrong. Did something happen to Larry?"

"No. It's not about him at all. It's about you. That's why I couldn't say anything on the phone. Larry told me you've been dating a teacher named Bill Forrest. Is that right?" He walked toward the kitchen. "You got any coffee?"

"Who I date's none of Larry's business. And what do you have to do with it?"

Alice followed him into the kitchen and poured two cups. Michael was a person who wouldn't be rushed.

He stared at his cup, holding it with both hands. "I shouldn't be telling you this. Remember that hit and run I told you about? The one involving the lawyer. Well, he's the prime suspect."

"Who?"

"Forrest. We think he killed Morse in revenge. Morse was the one who ran down his wife and kid about six years ago."

Alice's head snapped back.

"What do you mean? I don't believe he's capable of that."

"I know. That's our problem, too. We checked him out. Viet Nam vet. Decorated. Worst he's ever had is a speeding ticket. It doesn't seem to be in character for him. You knew about his wife and son?"

"I know they were killed by a drunk driver. Bill never went into details. I just thought it was too painful for him."

"Morse was drunk. He hit Forrest's wife and kid. Really bad. But he got the charge reduced. Paid a fine and got probation. After the trial, he moved to Waukegan to practice law."

"My God. Bill? A killer? He planned and carried out a murder?"

"Yeah. That's what we think. But there's no hard evidence to link him to the killing. Like I said, I shouldn't be telling you this, but I think you need to know. Not that I blame him, but he waited five years to do it. That's cold-blooded."

CHAPTER 55

▼

Alice worried about her date with Bill. She didn't want to let him know what she had learned.

Michael could be wrong. He admitted there wasn't any evidence. How do I get Bill to talk about it? I learned the hard way you never really know what another person's capable of. Wonder if I should wear the pants suit or body armor?

After showering, she rubbed lotion over her body, beginning with her shoulders and ending with her feet. Her drying skin drank in the cool moisture, like rain falling on parched desert sand. She imagined Bill, and then Gregory. He had been her first real love, that mind twitching, headlong rush, like water cascading over a cliff. She wondered if anyone really gets over their first passionate love.

"And now to get ready to go out with killer Bill," she said to her mirror image. "No. Suspected killer. I've got to think about my future. And Jason's." She pointed her fingers in the shape of a gun, and made a soft popping noise.

The late sun was tinting the undersides of the clouds with pink and lavender as Bill arrived at the door. He was nervous.

This is not just another date.

After three weeks, he thought it was time for their relationship to move to another level. He just didn't know if Alice was ready for the same thing. After a few moments, the door opened. Alice was dressed and waiting.

She reached out, took his hand and kissed him on the cheek. Then she dropped both hands to her sides as he walked in. Her usual warm hug and kiss had been replaced by a cool greeting.

"Hey, you look great, Alice."

"Thanks. Every woman needs to be flattered."

"I'm not just flattering you. I'm serious."

"Well, you look very good yourself. Want something to drink?" she said, continuing into the kitchen. She hesitated, and then asked, "Coke? Coffee?"

How could you kill someone?

"A glass of water, thanks." he said. It was as if this were their first date.

Maybe she's as concerned as I am that the time is right for us to end up in bed. After Alice gave some last minute instructions to Mrs. Garvey, they walked out toward Bill's maroon Pathfinder.

The night was cool, and only brightest stars were visible. A slight breeze swished through the trees.

He attempted to help her into the high seat. She turned her back to him and climbed in unassisted. She adjusted her seat belt and looked at the windshield.

I wish Michael had never told me about Morse.

As Bill climbed into the driver's seat, she thought of a car killing a person. "Well, then," said Bill as he settled in. "How about a nice Ethiopian restaurant?"

"Ethiopian?" asked Alice, surprised, looking at him for the first time in several minutes. "I didn't know there were any. Where's an Ethiopian restaurant around here?"

"Who said anything about around here?" The engine jumped to life and he put it in reverse. "There's a great place in Chicago, Mama Desta's. Ever been there?"

"Bill, the last few months, I've been happy just to come home and microwave dinner for me and Jason. Thank God for microwave cooking."

"Well, you're in for a surprise. The beer comes in quart bottles and there's no silverware."

The mention of beer sent a small shock wave pulsing through her. Everything conspired to make her more tense. She wanted to ask him how he could go on with his life as if nothing important had happened.

She wanted to tell him to stop and let her out. But she stared into the night hoping this darkness would provide her with answers. Her feelings were in conflict with her thoughts. She felt vulnerable.

"What do you mean 'no silverware'?"

"None. You eat everything with your fingers."

"Really?" She imagined people stuffing food into their mouths with their fingers, like Jason, food smeared around his mouth and face, and gobs dropping to the floor.

"Actually, you scoop up the food with pieces of a flat, bread-like thing that looks like a giant pancake."

She pictured Jason as a baby, sitting in his highchair, his face and hands covered with syrup.

"Well, I'll give it a try," she said, trying to sound enthusiastic.

"I do have a problem, though. With beer in quart bottles, I can never drink a whole one, so I'll need some help."

Alice smiled. "I'll be happy to help you there." Her mood lightened.

Not able to drink one liter of beer. After years of Larry's drinking, that's a trait I can appreciate.

As they drove down Skokie Highway, a police car came up behind them, lights flashing. Bill crossed two lanes and pulled off the road onto the shoulder. The car bounced across the dirt and rubble and skidded to a stop as the police car sped past.

Bill put his hands together at the top of the steering wheel and rested his head on his arms. "That was close."

"Bill, are you all right? They weren't after us. What's wrong?"

"Nothing. I'm okay. I just got a bit shaken, that's all.

CHAPTER 56

▼

Mama Desta's was a dark, store-front restaurant on Fullerton in a neighborhood that reeked of littered streets, homeless people, and very few places to park.

As they entered the restaurant, the pungent odor of smoke, beer, and exotic spices stung her nose. She recognized the aroma of curry.

After Bill ordered, Alice mentioned the heavy traffic on the streets. She hoped it would open the conversation to the topic foremost in her mind. Bill merely nodded and said nothing else. Then he reached across the table and took her hand. He asked her about work, and she told him about the new job that Gregory had offered her.

"It's really a step up for me. He hinted that I might be able to work on the KFC account if he gets it. But to start, I'll be trying to develop a strategy to help Manischewitz capture a bigger share of the snack cracker market.

"Is Gregory the one I met at the party?"

"Yes." Alice wondered what Gregory had said about her.

"Seems like a nice guy. You known him long? You seem to be old friends."

"Greg and I went to the same college. We had a few classes together. He was an art major, but we both took advertising courses." She was happy their food came.

"This food is really good," Alice said, as they scooped up the mounds of beans and pureed vegetables. "I'm glad you decided to split a beer with me. I don't know anyone except my ex who could drink a whole one of these."

"Heavy drinker?"

"Heavy?" she said between mouthfuls. "He was a full-blown alcoholic, but you didn't dare tell him that."

"Yeah. I had a friend who was an alcoholic. But he discovered AA years ago, and it saved his life."

"Well, I sure hope Larry does something. But I'm afraid he won't. I'll probably read about him in the paper some day. You know, 'Drunk Driver Dies in Accident.' I only hope he doesn't kill someone else." As soon as she said the words, she looked at Bill's face for a reaction.

"Oh, my God. I'm sorry, Bill."

"That's okay." A look of concern crossed his eyes, like the sweep of a search-light.

If Bill's wife and child were killed by a dunk driver as Michael said, the topic must be a sensitive one. Michael must be wrong.

After dinner, Bill drove down Fullerton, heading for the Biograph. Alice saw fewer brownstones and frame houses, and more large apartment buildings.

"We'll have to park in the lot across from the bank and cut through the little park. That can be a bit weird if you're not used to it. Just don't pay attention to anyone sleeping on the benches."

"Sounds like you've done this before."

"This's my area. I went to De Paul in the 70s. Had an apartment with three other guys over on Lill." He smiled, letting the memory of college days and summers at the beach wash away the thoughts of Morse.

CHAPTER 57

▼

Alice felt drained as they drove back to Lake Forest after the movie. "Beer, food, and a movie, and I'm ready for bed. I mean, it's just that I haven't been out this late for a long time."

The headlights reflected a man walking on the side of the highway. The thought of Bill's running him down flashed through Alice's mind.

"Can't imagine anyone out here at night," Bill commented.

The silence of the drive back was broken only by the "Blues Until Dawn" on NPR.

"Well, here we are," he said touching her arm softly.

"My God, I slept the whole way back. Not much company, am I. I'm not used to these late nights. Or should I say early mornings?"

"Hey, no problem. I'm glad you went with me. It's no fun doing things alone."

He helped her down from the car and put his arm around her shoulder as they walked toward the house. Alice found her key and put it into the lock. She turned and looked up into Bill's face. Then she rested her head against his chest, putting her arms around him.

"Thanks. I really had a wonderful time. Again. You know, after that disastrous breakfast, I didn't think I'd hear from you again."

"Really? I didn't think it was so disastrous."

"You know what I mean."

"Yeah." He kissed her. Holding her tightly, he was happy to feel her kissing him back.

"Want to come in for coffee?"

"Are you sure. It's late, and I promised George I'd help him clean out his garage tomorrow. Three cars and only room in the garage for one."

"Sounds like work. But you can leave from here, and be there in a few minutes." She couldn't believe the words came from her mouth. She opened the door, not looking at him.

CHAPTER 58

▼

Bill sat in the kitchen as Alice ground some fresh coffee. "We could have stopped at Starbuck's," he said. "You don't have to go to this trouble."

"It's no trouble." She poured water into the coffeemaker. "I enjoy it" She placed two plates and half an apple pie on the table. Bill sliced it into four pieces and put one piece of pie on each plate.

"I have to tell you, I'm a bit worried." She poured the coffee and sat down.

"The new job?"

"That's part of it. I start there in a week, and in addition to the new account, the Cheesie Spread account's coming with me."

"Well, that says something about your work. They must be happy to have you."

For a few minutes, they sat drinking coffee and eating pie in silence, not looking at each other.

There's no way he could be guilty of killing someone. Michael's wrong. It wouldn't be the first time. Two years ago, he was sure that sixteen-year-old had been guilty of burglary. Motive, he said. Needed money. Eye witness. But he'd been staying with friends in another town. The guilty person was the boy's cousin. Almost the same age. Looked enough like the boy to be his brother.

Bill reached across the table and took Alice's hand in his, rubbing the back of it with his thumb. "That pie was delicious. I'm glad you invited me in."

She leaned toward him. "I enjoy being with you."

"Me, too."

He was still holding her hand when she stood. She took a deep breath and let it out slowly. "C'mon," she said softly.

"What about Jason," Bill asked. "Won't my staying create a problem for him?"

"I don't think so, Bill. He's too young to really understand, and I think he likes you."

"Well, he did share a cookie with me Wednesday."

"That proves it. You're big with two year olds."

"And 35 year olds?"

"You are with this one."

Bill stood up, and Alice led him up to the master bedroom. Her heart was thumping as she turned on the light and dialed the dimmer down... "I'll be back in a moment." She walked into the bathroom, leaving him standing at the foot of the bed looking at the king size bed and the neat comforter. When he heard the bathroom door open, he turned.

Alice wore a red floral satin robe trimmed in soft pink. The material shimmered in the pale light. The faint scent of gardenias teased his nose. The contours of her body were clearly visible through the robe as she glided across the room. When she sat on the edge of the bed and crossed her legs, the robe opened slightly, showing her thigh.

She reached up and unbuttoned his shirt, pulling it out of his pants. He started to get aroused. He touched her face gently with his hand, cupping her cheek.

She took off his shirt and threw it behind her on the bed. It was like a scene from a movie, slow and sexy. She ran her fingers over his arms, reading the muscles, then pulling him toward her.

He took her face in both his hands and bent forward to kiss her. As he leaned toward her, he lost his balance, and had to lurch sideways onto the bed to avoid falling on top of her.

"This isn't the way it happens in the movies," he laughed, lying on his back. Alice pulled up the shoulder of the satin robe over her now exposed breast and laughed along with him. She got up, turned off the light, slipped off the robe and eased between the cool sheets, lying on her back. She heard the zipper of his pants and in a moment, felt him sliding in beside her. The darkness hid all their secrets.

The warmth of his body excited her even more, and she rolled to her side to face him. She touched his face, stroking his cheek and running her hand through his hair.

"The first time is so damned awkward, isn't it?" she said. "I'm afraid of saying or doing the wrong thing."

"It wouldn't be possible to say the wrong thing." He slipped his arm under her neck and pulled her toward him.

Alice put her head on his shoulder and caressed his chest. She kissed his ear, but as she moved her hand down toward his stomach, she felt his muscles tighten.

His hardness slipped away.

"Why don't we just lie here and hold each other. I'd like that, Bill. I'm too nervous to do anything."

But he couldn't relax. He felt the warmth of tears creep across his temples. He put his hand to his forehead, covering his eyes.

"What's wrong, Bill?"

As soon as she asked the question, Alice became fearful and tried to pull away, but he held her tightly.

He paused and took a breath. "I haven't been completely honest with you, Alice."

She started to breath rapidly, her face clutched to his chest, opening her mouth wide to suck in more air silently. Acid from the coffee rose to her throat.

He has a commitment to someone else. He's got herpes. Or AIDS.

She lay next to him, naked, exposed, vulnerable. She pulled free and sat up, holding the blanket and crossing her arms in front of her breasts.

"What's wrong?" The story Michael told her came crashing through her mind.

She bit her lip to keep from shouting that she knew all about Morse. After several seconds of silence, she finally mumbled, "You're a...you're married, aren't you."

"No." His voice was so quiet she could hardly hear.

"I need to know what's going on here. I have a right to know. I invite you into my house, into my bed. I want to know." There was a quiver in her abdomen. She retrieved her robe from the floor and slipped her arms in, wrapping it around herself. Then she stood and faced him.

He paused. "I was responsible for their deaths."

"Whose deaths?"

"Marisa and Andrew. I caused them to die."

Alice was quiet, absorbing the information.

"You told me they were killed in an accident."

"That's true." He sat up, leaning against the wall and wiping his eyes with his hands. After he pulled the blanket up to his chest, he took a breath and continued. "It happened when I was teaching at Roosevelt High School. I was supposed to pick up Andrew from his music lesson. Some students came in to get some help on a paper, so I called my wife to pick him up. She got there late. If I had picked him up when I was supposed to, everything would have been okay." He paused and took another deep breath. When he continued, his voice quavered, "He was only nine."

Alice crawled in bed next to him, and put her arms around his head, pulling him as close as she could.

"It's okay, Bill," she whispered, "it's okay. You can talk about it if you want to," she said. "I can understand." She thought about losing Jason to a drunk driver The anger scared her.

"No, you have a right to know everything," said Bill. "Especially now. I should have told you up front, but I wanted to wait until the right time. I guess this must be the right time."

Alice, her robe still wrapped tightly about her, allowed him to lie back, and she sat cross legged facing him. She reached down and took his hand in both of hers, feeling his pain oozing into her through his fingers.

"After the funeral," he continued, "I kinda went crazy. Took a leave of absence and started traveling."

"Where'd you go?"

"I just hit the road. Had to get away. You don't realize how easy is to become homeless. I was gone for almost a year, doing odd jobs to get money for food. I stayed away from cities and lived in a tent or my truck. Then one morning in the Rocky Mountains, I watched the sun rise and felt the pain had subsided enough for me to come back home."

It was also the day I decided to kill Robert Morse.

He slid back down under the covers and Alice scooted under with him, putting her head on his chest. Slipping his arm around her back again, he pulled her to him and held her. "Actually, the wilderness helped, and being alone for so long. I came to terms with the incident as best I could."

"I'm sorry, Bill. I wish there was something I could say. What ever happened to the drunk driver?"

"He was a lawyer. He got off with a slap on the wrist. Paid his fine and walked away."

"That's terrible."

"Well, life's pretty ironic. He was killed a few years ago in a hit and run accident. He got what he deserved."

"How did that make you feel?"

"That justice had been done. The police questioned me. They thought I might have done it." He sat up. There was no need for her to know the truth. *What she doesn't know, she can't tell anyone.* He looked at her intently in the dim light. "I wish I had. But that's enough about my miserable past. This's a hell of a conversation for two people in bed for the first time." He pulled her to him and kissed her on the forehead, squeezing her hard enough to make her exhale involuntarily.

Alice didn't know what to believe. Michael believed Bill had killed Morse. But Bill had just told her he didn't. She had always heard that people who lie can't meet you eye to eye. But Bill looked right at her when he told her.

"It's okay, Bill." She put her finger on his lips "We'll have lots of other times. When you first started telling me the story, I imagined all kinds of things. I thought you were going to tell me you were married. Or that you had AIDS or something." She pulled his head to her chest, held him as tightly as he had held her. She stroked his head, soothing him as if he were a little child who had just hurt his finger. She heard the muffled barking of a dog, asking to come in where it was warm. She realized she was falling in love.

CHAPTER 59

▼

A week after their first night in bed together, Bill went to the College of Lake County English office to examine the syllabi of previous courses. Taking several courses of study from the files, he walked down the blue corridor to the library. He pushed through the turnstile, found an empty table, and spread out.

He absently wrote Alice's name on the blank paper in front of him as he read through the first syllabus. He wrote it once, twice. He put a box around it. Alice Solinsky. Thoughts of her swirled through his mind.

He picked up a syllabus and turned to the poetry selections. There were several contemporary poets, including MeKeel McBride. He was unfamiliar with her work, and he turned to the text to read some of her poems.

McBride. That was Alice's married name. McBride.

"Shit!" Several students at the next table to looked up. He smiled at them and apologized. He looked through his wallet and found Detective Don Walker's card. At the bottom of the card on the left it said Waukegan Police Department. And on the right it said Michael McBride, Chief of Detectives,

He went to the phone at the desk and called the number on the card.

"Detective Division. May I help you?"

"Michael McBride, please."

"Who's calling?"

"His brother."

"Larry? You in some trouble again? Michael's in a meeting right now. You leave a number and he'll call you back. He worries about you."

"Yeah. I know. I'll get back to him. Thanks." Bill replaced the phone on the cradle. He collected his things, and left.

CHAPTER 60

▼

Larry McBride left the Greenleaf Sports bar in Park City sometime after two in the AM. He staggered toward his truck and climbed in He opened the quart bottle of Budweiser in the paper bag on the seat. After taking a drink, he put the bottle between his legs and started the truck.

He liked drinking at the Greenleaf, because it was a short drive to his garage, where he often slept. He held tightly to the steering wheel, afraid he'd float to the roof of the truck if he didn't. Squinting into the night, he wondered why everyone had their bright lights on. Dividing his attention between the few other cars and speedometer, he kept in the right-hand lane, alternating between 50 and 65. When he reached 22nd street the light was green. He made the long right curving turn on Buckley Road, and turned left on Sheridan, feeling safe.

The new halogen streetlights blazed brilliantly, but everything was dark to Larry. He passed Arden Shore. He passed North. He passed his garage at Scranton. He passed Witchwood. With a whiplash jump, he opened his eyes. A car was stalled in the road at McKinley. As he passed Hawthorn, he hit the brake. He was flying toward the stopped car at sixty miles an hour.

CHAPTER 61

▼

Alice left Varonian and Varonian early on the worst Friday she could remember. A power outage had knocked out computers and phone lines for over an hour. Gregory and Jean were in New York on vacation over the 4th of July, and Nishan refused to make final decisions on any of Gregory's projects. One account executive on her Cheesie Spread team quit without notice, saying she and her boyfriend had split up and she was moving to San Francisco. All Alice could think about was a long soak in the tub and a relaxing evening with Bill. The thought of his being a killer had almost disappeared from her mind. As she made dinner for Jason, she noticed the message light flashing on her phone.

"This message is for Alice McBride. Please call Highland Park Hospital emergency room regarding the accident involving your husband, Larry."

Alice picked up the phone and dialed the number. After getting to the right department, she requested information on Larry.

"This is Alice Solinsky. I was Alice McBride. What's going on? I'm not married to Larry McBride any more."

The dispassionate voice continued. "There's been an accident involving your husband, Larry McBride. A police ambulance brought him in."

"But we're divorced."

"Well, we got your name and phone number from his insurance."

"How bad was he hurt?"

"I really can't discuss that over the phone. You need to come down to the hospital and talk to the doctor. Mr. McBride needs surgery. Is there any other family member we can contact?"

"He has a brother, Michael. He's a detective for the Waukegan Police Department. What kind of surgery?"

"I'm sorry, you'll have to discuss that with Doctor Birmingham."

After she hung up, Alice felt angry. *Why do I have to be called? Why do I have to be the one to take care of things.* She dialed Michael's home number. His answering machine responded. Michael could be on an assignment or could have gone away for the long weekend. There was no way to know. She left a message for him.

She walked back to the bathroom and turned off the water. It was a little after five, and Bill was supposed to come over at 7:30. She called him.

"There's been an accident. No, I'm all right and Jason's fine. It's Larry. I'm sure he was DUI again, and this time it's serious. I tried calling his brother, but there's no answer. I'm going over to Highland Park Hospital. Larry needs some kind of surgery. He screwed up my life when we were married, and now he's doing it again. Damn him!"

"Alice," Bill said. "You all right? Is there anything I can do? You want me to go there with you? I could pick you up, or meet you there."

"No, I think it's better if I go alone. No sense both of us wasting an evening. I'm sorry."

"Hey, no big deal. I'll meet you there at the hospital. Then we can eat later, if you feel up to it."

"Thanks. You know, you really don't have to." She hoped he would insist, but she didn't want Bill to think that Larry might somehow stride back into her life. "Just talking to you makes me feel calmer."

"It's a big hospital. Did they say what part he was in?"

"They said the surgical unit, but I don't know where that is."

"I'll find it. See you there."

Alice hung up the phone, thinking she was lucky to have someone as understanding as Bill. Grabbing her purse, she went next door to get Mrs. Garvey.

Bill might not be as understanding if he knew about me and Gregory.

At the hospital, the doctor on duty told Alice what happened.

"The head trauma was bad enough to cause a concussion," said the doctor. "And he apparently had an open beer bottle between his legs. The bottle broke when it hit the steering wheel. He was cut pretty badly on his right leg and his groin. He's a lucky man. If his femoral artery had been cut, he could have bled to death in a few minutes. He registered a .18 alcohol level. We don't know if he passed out before the accident or as a result of the head trauma. In any event, he's going to require surgery to repair a partially severed groin muscle on his right leg, and some stitches on his penis and testicles, which were lacerated."

How many times I've wished just such a problem on his sex organs.

"How bad is his leg, Doctor? I mean, what about walking?"

"He should regain the full use of his leg." The doctor continued, almost as if he had memorized a speech. "As far as his sex life is concerned, there will be some pain for a while, but probably no long term lack of function."

"Well, as often as we had sex the last year we were married," said Alice, "I wouldn't have noticed. But there may be some old girl friends who might be a little pissed," she said, putting her hand in front of her mouth to keep from laughing. "But what about the concussion?"

"Since there's no skull fracture or evidence of inter-cranial bleeding, we're keeping him sedated overnight to give the swelling time to reduce."

"Is there something I can do?" she asked.

"Actually, no. I shouldn't even be telling you all this. If you were still married, I'd have you sign the surgery consent. We may be able to have him do it himself. We'll try to locate his brother. You might as well go home. There's not much you can do here."

She looked up and saw Bill turning the corner. He waved. She walked quickly toward him, and allowed herself to be swallowed up in his embrace. As soon as she felt his arms, she went limp.

"C'mon, you look like a lost puppy. You need some dinner." He turned her toward the door and guided her with his arm firmly around her shoulders. "You can tell me about the problem in the car."

She explained what had happened. "I almost laughed when the doctor told me everything. Is that sick, or what? His brother Michael's a detective, and they don't get along. Michael's the one who'll have to sign for the surgery, if they can find him. I can't believe they called me. I'm the last one he'd want."

Alice was worried for Larry, who was the only father Jason had ever known. Larry had taken his fatherly role seriously after the divorce. When he visited, he was always sober, and several times took care of Jason when Alice had to work on a weekend. He even took Jason for a day when Alice and Bill wanted to get away. She started crying when they pulled into the driveway. Bill helped her out of the car, and she leaned on him as they walked up to the door.

"Is she okay?" asked Mrs. Garvey, as they entered the house.

"Yeah, but she's exhausted. It's been a hell-of-a day."

"If you don't mind my asking, how's Larry?"

"He needs surgery, but he'll be okay."

"Well, I'm going home to bed myself. It's too late for an old lady to be up. I'll be around tomorrow if you need me."

"Thanks, Mrs. Garvey."

Bill helped Alice up the stairs to the bedroom.

"Thanks." She sat on the edge of the bed. "I don't know what happened. Guess I've been going on adrenaline, and it just ran out. Can you stay? I won't hear Jason if he wakes up."

"Sure. I was planning to stay whether you asked me or not. If you want, I can sleep downstairs on the sofa."

"No you don't. I want you right here next to me."

The next morning, Alice awoke to the sound of voices downstairs. Slipping on her robe, she walked downstairs to find Bill and Jason at the kitchen table, eating oatmeal.

"That looks good," she said. "Mmm. Brown sugar and raisins, too."

"More inna pot, mommy. I'm stuffed." He patted his stomach and smiled at Bill.

When Jason went in the living room to watch cartoons, Alice sat down and called the hospital.

"Well, the surgery's scheduled for this morning. Larry's brother signed the consent. One day, Larry's going to kill himself with his drinking."

The mention of Michael made Bill wonder if he could trust her with his life. "I'm sure the surgery'll go well. He's lucky it's not life and death surgery." He paused and nodded his head in Jason's direction. "Does he know?"

The question caught Alice off guard. For a moment, she felt the squeeze of panic. When she looked at Bill's face, she realized he was asking about the accident.

"No. I'll tell him when everything's calmed down a bit."

"Don't wait too long."

"Let me handle it, Bill. I can take care of it." She paused, realizing how that sounded. "Sorry. I'm pretty edgy."

Alice knew eventually she would have to tell Bill everything. If their relationship was to progress, she could have no secrets from him. Secrets are like a speck of mold on bread. You don't notice the inconspicuous spot. One day you reach for a slice and the whole loaf is contaminated.

CHAPTER 62

▼

A few days later, Gregory called Alice into his office.

"I called Larry. He sounds pretty good, considering," he said.

"You going by to see him?"

"Can't. I'm swamped here and I may have to fly out to New York again."

"I'm going by this afternoon. I'll tell him you send your regards."

Gregory sat behind an immense desk cluttered with paper. Anyone listening to their conversation would never have guessed they had once been intimate, or that Gregory and Larry were more than casual acquaintances. The friendship between them had faded. Gregory had become afraid of Larry's heavy drinking.

Alice turned to leave.

"Is there any problem?" Gregory asked.

"What do you mean?"

"You know, with Larry. And Jason."

"You mean does he suspect? You mean would I tell him that you're Jason's father? You mean would I do anything to make you take responsibility?" Alice felt her face turn warm.

"No. I mean with the business and all…"

"Don't worry you son-of-a-bitch. You can relax." Her fingers crumpled the paper she held in her hand.

"Sorry I asked," Gregory muttered looking at the crushed paper.

Alice turned abruptly and left the office.

Same old Gregory. Always thinking about himself, always backing away from a problem.

CHAPTER 63

▼

Alice left work an hour early to visit Larry at the hospital. He was now up on crutches, and had been moved to a room adjacent to the exit door, down the hall from the nurses' station.

The duty nurse asked her to wait while a nurse's aid changed Larry's bandages. Alice stood outside, listening to their voices which slipped easily through the partially open door.

"Well, I'll be good as new pretty soon. You'll have to let me take you out to dinner. Or something." Alice could see Larry's boyish grin.

"I don't think so, Mr. McBride."

"Hey, call me Larry. You're the only woman who has touched me there that I haven't slept with."

"Oh. What about your mother?" asked the aid.

"Never knew her."

"Oh. You can put your robe back on and stand up if you want."

"I will be OK in that department, won't I? I mean, I'll still be able to, you know, uh, perform, won't I?"

"Oh, sure. Your prognosis is very good. Once the stitches are removed, you'll be good as new."

"Say, Phyllis, I got a question. What's this A plus on my wrist band next to my name?"

"That's your blood type, A positive."

"Yeah? You sure? I thought I was B positive. I mean, that's what the hospital told my ex-wife.

Alice moved closer to the open door. The warm air from the room caressed her cheek, making her skin feel dry. The nurse at the station looked at her and grimaced, wondering what she was doing.

"Well, Mr. McBride, the lab ran the tests twice because you needed a unit of blood after the surgery. So I think the band is right. In an emergency, that could have been dangerous. Why did you think you had B positive blood?" Deceit squeezed the breath out of Alice's body.

"My son had a problem after he was born and needed surgery, and there was a chance he'd need blood, so me and Alice, that was my wife, went to the blood bank, you know. Alice took care of the paperwork. She said she was O and me and Jason was B positive."

"Well, there's a mistake somewhere, Mr. McBride. You're A positive, and that's for sure. And if your wife is O, your son can't have B positive blood."

"You sure?"

"I worked in a blood lab for two years. That's something I know. How do you know son's B positive?"

"I seen his records. And you sure I got A positive."

"No doubt about it. That's what we gave you, and you're doing fine. If you want, you can talk to the doctor about it. He'll be able to answer your questions this evening."

The aid left the room in time to see Alice's back. Alice couldn't think of anything Larry could do in his condition, and by the time he got out of the hospital, she hoped to think of something.

That night, her phone rang several times, but she didn't answer it.

When the phone rang at work the next morning, she was surprised to hear Larry's voice.

"How did you get this number?"

"Never mind how I got it. I got to talk to you Alice. It's important."

"Larry, I just can't drop everything and run over there. I need to go to the cleaners after work and pick up something for dinner."

"Just tell Billy schoolteacher to eat out tonight." He was speaking rapidly, loudly. "This is important. And don't bring Jason."

Alice was shocked. Why would he tell her not to bring Jason, as if she had any intention of doing so.

"Well, you gonna come by or not?"

Years of conditioning came crashing down on her. "OK. OK," she responded finally. "I'll be there as soon as I can."

CHAPTER 64

▼

A little past six that evening, Alice walked into Larry's room. A male nurse was writing the information on the aluminum encased chart. The nurse nodded to Alice and then turned to go.

"Wait a minute, Alfredo. I want you to meet my ex-wife, Alice."

"Good to meet you, señora."

Alice looked at Alfredo, a muscular young man with dark skin and black hair and eyes. She walked toward the bed and stopped at the foot. Alfredo replaced the chart and started for the door, checking the rubber gloves as he passed the dispenser. "Now, what's this big important news that you had to tell me?"

"News? I never said nothing about news. But I got a question for you. I want to know who's Jason's father, 'cause I ain't, and you know it." He yelled to Alfredo, who was walking out the door. "Tell her, Alfredo."

Alfredo turned around. "I don't understand, señor. What you mean? Tell her what?"

"Look at my chart, Alfredo. What's my blood type?"

Alfredo returned and picked up the chart, flipping through several pages. "You have A positive blood."

"Tell her what that means, Alfredo. Tell her what the fuck that means." Larry's voice became so loud that the shift nurse came into the room. She was a large, heavy woman with the smell of clean starched linen mixed with antiseptic.

"Is everything all right here?" she asked, her voice deep and demanding.

"Everything is fine," shouted Larry. "Alfredo is just gonna tell this slut why her kid can't be my kid."

The room became suddenly silent, as if everyone took a breath at the same time. The nurse looked at Alfredo.

"I think they need you in 12B," she said. Alice started to cry. Alfredo gave the nurse a momentary puzzled look, then nodded his head and handed her the chart. He walked outside the room, jogged to the nurse's station, and then returned and stood in the hall where he could not be seen.

"I think you had better leave," the nurse said to Alice, putting her hand on Alice's shoulder, and turning her in the direction of the door, pushing her gently. Wiping her eyes, she nodded her head and turned toward the door.

"You're goddam right she better leave," Larry shouted, his voice rising in pitch. He started to cough, and he rolled to get out of bed.

"Calm down, Mr. McBride. You'll hurt yourself." The nurse walked to his bedside, blocking him from leaving the bed.

"Get the hell out of my way," he said pushing at her. She grabbed his wrist, turning him toward her. Alfredo ran back into the room and grabbed Larry's other arm.

"No," Larry shouted. He twisted his head toward Alice as she continued to back slowly toward the door. "Don't you leave, godammit. I want an answer. I got a right to know. Who's the father? I got a right to know," Larry shouted toward the ceiling, held down on his back.

Tears streaming down her face, Alice stood in the doorway, wiping her eyes. "Gregory," she whispered through her tears, looking at the floor. Then she raised her head, and sneered, narrowing her eyes as if she were pointing a knife. "Gregory! Your good friend, Gregory!" she shouted.

"You're a goddamned liar," Larry screamed, his face contorted into a grimace to prevent the tears from flowing. Larry writhed like a snake caught in a sack, wrenching his arm from Alfredo and screamed, a crazed wolf-like howl. He scooped the bed-pan off the small table and threw it at Alice. It clanged as it hit the door and bounced to the floor. "I'll kill him, the son-of-a-bitch. And I'll kill you, too. At that moment, two other orderlies entered and helped Alfredo tie Larry's arms to the bed rails with gauze restraints. As soon as he was quiet for a moment, the nurse injected him with a sedative and then ushered Alice out the door.

Walking back to her car, tears still streaming down her cheeks, Alice berated herself. She had always thought one day she would tell him the truth.

Why'd it have to be like this? Why'd he have to learn this way?

CHAPTER 65

▼

When she got home from the hospital, Alice called Bill. Crying, she asked him to come over.

He felt an almost electrical tension as he entered the house.

She was sitting on the sofa, legs folded, rocking back and forth.

"My God, Alice, what's wrong? You all right?"

Sobbing so she could barely stand, Alice threw her arms around his neck He held her tightly, almost lifting her off the ground, afraid she would collapse if he let go. When her sobs ceased, she wiped her face with the palms of her hands. Her eyes were red and puffy, and there were black smudges on her cheeks. Suddenly, she pulled away and threw herself face down on the sofa.

"Oh, God, what have I done?" She felt like vomiting, and swallowed hard, holding back the ball in her stomach that pushed to get out. The pain in her stomach eased. She sat, head in her hands, elbows on her knees. "I'm glad you came, Bill. I've been going crazy since I left the hospital. I don't know what to do. I can't think. I didn't want him to find out. Or you either. I swear, I was going to tell him, but not like this."

"Didn't want who to find out what? What didn't you want me to find out?" He paused. "The best thing to do when you can't think is don't think. Catch your breath, and I'll make some tea." When she started to cry again, he held her for several minutes. Then he helped her up and led her to the kitchen, pulling her by the hand like a petulant child. She rested her elbows on the table and put her head in her hands again, wiping her eyes with a napkin from the holder.

He turned on the soft light over the stove, its dim light casting long, weak shadows, and found some chamomile tea.

She imagined the conversation each time she thought of telling him.

Hey, Bill, this might sound silly, but I got drunk and was raped by my ex-lover while I was married to Larry. I got pregnant and let Larry think the child was his. You see, this guy and I lived together in college, and he got me pregnant then, too, but I had an abortion just before I graduated. His name? Gregory. Couldn't you guess?"

If it hadn't been real life, it would sound like a bad soap opera.

"Can I fix you something? Scrambled eggs and toast."

"If I ate anything now, I'd vomit."

He brought the two cups of tea to the table and sat down across from her. She took a few sips of the chamomile tea and slumped back in the chair, closing her eyes.

"Bill, I need to talk or I'll explode." Her eyes started to fill with tears as she spoke, but she dabbed them with another napkin. She wanted to reach out and take his hand, but she grasped the table-top instead. "Remember when you told me about your past, how your wife and son died?" she sobbed. "And I said I understood? I understood how you felt about Morse. I wanted to tell you how I understood, but I couldn't. I wouldn't blame you if you walk out of here and never come back."

"I don't understand. What're you talking about?"

Alice looked away. When he reached across the table to put his hand on her arm, she pulled back. She stood up. Her legs trembled, but she straightened herself. She walked to the sink, wet her hand, and patted her face. She couldn't tell him and look at him at the same time.

"Wait a minute. Oh, my God. It's Larry," he exclaimed. "Now I understand."

Alice nodded and continued. "But how did you know?"

"I'm sorry. I thought Larry was doing well."

"He is."

"Then what are we talking about?"

"It isn't Larry. It's Jason." Alice looked out the window into the graying day. "Larry isn't Jason's father."

"You mean you were married before?"

"No." She shook her head slowly, holding on the sink edge for support.

"I'm confused. I don't understand what you're talking about."

"After Larry and I had been married almost four years, I got pregnant."

"You're sure it wasn't Larry's?"

"Yes."

"How can you be so sure?"

"When Jason turned up with B positive blood, I knew who the father was."

Alice recounted how she and Gregory had met in college and lived together for two years.

"Then just before we graduated, I found out I was pregnant. We broke up. Gregory didn't know about the pregnancy."

"What did you do?"

"I had an abortion. I was still in the first trimester, so it was uneventful."

Bill looked at the woman he had been dating and sleeping with, the hard-working mother, the tender sensitive woman.

"So you had an abortion. I've always been in favor of abortion, in certain circumstances, and that sounds like one of them. Lots of women have abortions. That's not so terrible. And it was years ago."

"About three years ago, Gregory and I ran into each other again when he moved to Lake Forest." She walked back to the table and sat across from Bill. "He discovered Larry's Garage was where he took his cars." The story was becoming easier to tell. She recounted it like a movie she had seen, looking from the stove to the refrigerator. "After the housewarming, Larry was hooked by Gregory's wealth. All he could talk about was his friendship with Gregory." Alice told about the fishing trip, and her subsequent dinner with Gregory. "I had too much to drink, and he took me to his studio and took advantage of my condition. I could call it rape, but who'd believe that? I mean I was in his place and I was drunk. The end result is I got pregnant. Again."

"But how'd Larry find out after all this time?"

"After his accident, he learned his true blood type, and when he confronted me at the hospital, I told him the truth."

"My God. And he never suspected?"

"After I got pregnant, there wasn't any reason to tell him."

"But Gregory, of all people. And now you're working for him?"

"Weird, huh. One mistake, and I get a lifetime to repent. Not that I regret Jason. He's the reason I'm working for Gregory. Money. Gregory offered me a substantial raise over what I was making before."

"How can you stand seeing him every day?"

"Like I said, the money."

"But why'd he even offer you the job?"

"Maybe it was guilt. I don't know. I don't even see him much at work. He travels a lot." She paused. "I know what you must be thinking. But I'll tell you something I know you'll understand. One of the things that holds my life together is Jason. I may have done something a little crazy, but that's okay. I have Jason."

Bill could only shake his head.

They sat in silence for several minutes. The room darkened as night approached.

Bill knew her life wasn't the only one that was weird. But he decided against saying anything about Morse's death. What she didn't know, she couldn't tell her ex-brother-in-law. He wasn't aware that she was just getting warmed up. When she told him about Gregory's affair with Jean, he sat up in his chair, surprised again.

"His wife?" Bill asked incredulous.

"She's the one who broke us up in college."

"And he raped you three years ago, and now you work for him? You're right. It's weird. But you've had a rough time. I can understand Larry's anger and frustration. The love he had for Jason was torn to shreds. He had a son, and then he didn't have a son. He still loves him even though he doesn't want to. And poor Jason."

Alice shook her head. "What am I going to do?"

"I don't know, Alice. I really don't know. Maybe you can talk to Larry when he gets out of the hospital. He's in pain now, what with the accident and the shock of finding out."

"Mommy?" a little voice called from halfway down the stairs. "I'm hungry."

"My God, I forgot about dinner. Want to go to McDonald's?"

"What happened to Daddy? Did he get hurt?"

"Have you been listening to us?" Alice looked at Bill. "What do I say?" she whispered. "What can I tell him?"

"Tell him the truth. It's always the best way."

Jason came down the stairs, slowly, as if he were going toward something he didn't want to be near. The rough soles of his feet pajamas scuffed across the carpet. He stopped next to the arm of the sofa, holding a stuffed puppy in his hand. She took him in her arms and moved to the sofa, where she sat him on her lap.

"A bad thing happened, Jason. Daddy got hurt in an accident, but he's all right."

"Is he hurt bad, Mommy?"

"He had to go to the hospital to get fixed up. But he'll be all right."

"I want to see him." He started to cry, and Alice put his head on her shoulder and cried with him. "Tell you what, Jason," Alice said. "Let's go and have dinner at McDonald's and you can sleep in my bed tonight? How's that?"

"But I want to see daddy."

"I know. Maybe we can visit him tomorrow. Would you like a glass of chocolate milk before we go?"

Alice went into the kitchen and poured the milk. Jason followed her and kneeled on his chair, waiting for her to pour the chocolate syrup into his glass. As he started drinking, she returned to Bill in the living room.

"I'm going to stick around this weekend in case you need me." He hoped she would refuse.

"There's no need to cancel your camping trip. I know it's important for you. It's Thursday, and you'll be back Monday." Alice was glad he was going. There were some things she needed to do, and Bill's absence would give her the chance to do them.

"Why don't you and Jason come with me. It might help you."

"No, there are things I have to take care of here."

"Well, I'll leave a number where I can be reached. I can be back in a few of hours if you need anything."

As Bill drove toward North Kettle Moraine, he wondered if there was a future in his relationship with Alice.

CHAPTER 66

▼

When Larry was discharged from Highland Park Hospital he was met by Michael, who felt obligated to help his younger brother. As an adolescent, Larry resented Michael's help. When Larry and some of his young high school friends were accused of stealing a car and joy-riding, Michael, as a young police officer, was the one who managed to get the charge reduced to a misdemeanor. When Larry was arrested for drunk driving at age 20, Michael was the one who posted bail and spoke to the judge.

It wasn't until Larry bought his own garage that he felt that he had accomplished something all his own.

Now the old frustrations bubbled to the surface, like soup scum to the top of a boiling pot. Larry bristled at his need to be taken care of. When Michael tried to help him into the car, Larry pulled his arm away and almost fell. Michael's assistance was met with silence for the entire 30 minute drive to Michael's home.

"There's no need to get so angry for crissakes. I'm just trying to help."

"I know. It's just this whole mess. I feel so goddam helpless."

"I can imagine. But you can stay at my place for a week or so until you get back to normal. Then you can do whatever you want. The doctor said you really shouldn't be alone."

"So what're you gonna do? Quit your job and take care of me?"

"At least I'll be here evenings. During the day, you can watch TV or something."

"And who's gonna take care of the garage?"

"You know Eddie can handle things. He's been doing all right so far. Call him up. I'll take you by there now if you want."

Larry learned how to maneuver on crutches, which was not as easy as it looked. He was limited to the first floor, which meant sleeping on the sofa. He hurt when he moved, and he hurt when he sat. The only comfortable position was flat on his back with both his head and bandaged leg elevated on pillows.

Each day he fed the small flame of his fury against Gregory and Alice. Small twigs at first, then larger, until it became a conflagration that engulfed him.

CHAPTER 67

▼

One morning Larry dragged himself up the stairs to Michael's bedroom. He sat on the edge of Michael's bed and with a screwdriver, he pried open the locked drawer in Michael's desk. The tool left ugly white scratches and gouges in the dark wood, but Larry was unconcerned. He knew he'd find a pistol, and he smiled as he looked into the drawer. There were two. He removed the .45 automatic and ran his finger along the flat side of the barrel, touching the letters and numbers tenderly. Colt above, M1A11913 below. Series 70. The clip was empty, and he didn't have the time to look for bullets. He put it back and picked up the other, much smaller pistol. A .38 Rossi 274 with a two inch barrel. The cylinder had a full five rounds. It would do nicely. Not as powerful, but it would intimidate anyone he aimed it at. Then he hopped down the stairs. At each jolt, his body shook, sending waves of pain shooting from his groin through his leg. He rested a moment half-way down, holding the handrail and waiting for the throbbing to subside. After resting again at the bottom of the stairs, he put the pistol in a denim canvas bag with his hospital papers and called a taxi.

He boarded the train for Chicago. Today he was neither happy nor sad. He was moving through space toward a conclusion, but he wasn't sure what kind. He watched the scenery fly by, from the boarded up bungalows of North Chicago and Great Lakes to the affluent mansions of Glencoe and Wilmette.

Larry remembered the first time he jumped off a high dive, being suspended in air, hitting the water. Mostly, he remembered the queasy feeling in his stomach as he fell. He had the same feeling now.

When he left the train at Union Station, he climbed the stairs one at a time, and set out down Jackson Street toward the Prudential Building on Michigan, which housed the offices of Varonian and Varonian. He had no idea how long it would take him, but he didn't care. His bag, which hung from a shoulder strap, swung back and forth as he hobbled down the street on his crutches. At Jackson and Sherman, he stopped and rested, leaning against a brick wall next to a construction dumpster. His head ached and he was hot and sweaty.

A few people looked at him as they passed, but most looked away. He reached in his bag shuffled through papers, found his bottle of Oxaprozin, and threw it in the dumpster.

Anti-inflammatory, my ass. It's a steroid. All the years I lifted weights I never took steroids, and I ain't gonna start now. What I need is a beer. The doctor had said no alcohol till I finished my medication. Well, I'm through with it now.

It was after eleven o'clock. He looked for a bar. He was thirsty and hungry, too. He hadn't eaten all day and he hadn't had a drink since he'd gone into the hospital. Michael had taken all the alcohol out of the house. He crossed State Street, and then at Wabash, he saw Charley's Tavern. Two hours later, he felt much better.

Sweat dampened his shirt by the time he arrived at The Prudential Building although the summer day was cooled by a breeze from the lake. The air conditioning chilled him as he checked the directory before he rode the elevator up to the seventh floor. In the three years he had known Gregory Varonian, this was Larry's first visit to the offices of Varonian and Varonian.

CHAPTER 68

▼

The same day, Alice sat at her desk staring at the phone. She worked up the nerve to call Michael's number, hoping to talk to Larry for the first time since she admitted Jason was Gregory's son. She left a message on the machine and then called the garage. Eddie answered.

"I ain't seen him since Michael brung him down here, gotta be three, four days ago. I tell you, he ain't doing too good on them crutches. Slipped on some oil when he was here. Almost fell down."

"Thanks, Eddie. If you see him, tell him I called."

Alice was frightened. She had never seen Larry so enraged. Maybe Larry was sleeping, or didn't feel like answering Michael's phone.

As she walked back to her desk from the coffee maker in the back room, she heard the commotion in the reception area. The outer office door banged against the wall. The glass hissed like a rattlesnake.

"I want to see that son-of-a-bitch Varonian."

Alice recognized the voice instantly. She froze for a moment. Unable to see around the corner, she quietly tiptoed to the end of the short corridor and stood next to the small conference room. Hidden by a partition and a large planter, she watched in horror as Larry hobbled up to the receptionist and leaned over her desk, balancing on one leg and his crutches, repeating his demand.

The young receptionist pushed her chair back from her desk, her eyes as wide as her glasses. The unmistakable stench of beer and cigarettes filled the small area.

"Tell him Larry McBride is here," he shouted. The receptionist started to say something, but Larry reached over the desk, knocking papers and the plastic correspondence basket to the floor along with the phone. "Just do it!" He braced himself on the desk to keep from falling.

The receptionist picked up the phone and touched a button on the intercom. "Mr. Varonian, there's a Mr. Larry McBride is here to see you." Her voice was high pitched and trembling.

"Tell him to get his ass out here or I'll go there and drag him out," continued Larry, hardly waiting for her to finish.

Two blue business-suited employees walked into the reception area from the office behind where Alice stood and looked at Larry.

"Is there a problem?" asked one.

"What the hell're you looking at? G'wan back to work. This ain't got nothing to do with you." He held his crutch like a sword in one hand. They backed up.

The receptionist lifted the phone. Larry put his hand on the disconnect bar.

"Just leave it alone and sit there."

She pulled her mini-skirt hem toward her knees.

Alice stood cringing behind the partition. She didn't know whether to come out or stay where she was. She knew what he was capable of. He almost killed an employee who tried to steal five thousand dollars from him. Larry put him in the hospital with several broken ribs, and a cracked cheekbone.

She was humiliated and fearful for herself, so she remained hidden, hoping Larry would think she was at lunch.

Moments later, Gregory walked up to her. It amazed her that he could look so calm.

She whispered, "Get back into your office and call 911. He's crazy."

"Don't worry, I can handle this."

She watched the scene unfold, like a spectacle in slow motion, praying silently that nothing would happen.

As Gregory approached from behind Larry, he spoke rapidly. "Larry, how're you doing? Glad you're finally out of the hospital. Alice told me what a rough time you've had."

"Yeah, I bet she did," Larry muttered, turning his head toward Gregory.

"And what're you doing here? I think this is the first time you've been to the offices up here.

"Listen, you asshole, I ought to just kill you right now." He turned on his one good leg.

Alice relaxed for a moment, seeing Larry sway. He seemed to be in no condition to do much of anything.

Gregory stopped abruptly, as if he had just walked into a glass wall. Several other people had been drawn into the corridor and stood near Alice, watching and whispering. Alice hoped no one knew Larry was her ex-husband. She told one of the men to call security on the direct line.

"Hold on, Larry. What's going on here? What're you talking about?"

"Where is she? Where is that cheating bitch?"

"Who?"

"Don't gimme that shit."

Alice could see Larry's face. His eyes were wide open. She could see the whites surrounding his pupils. He leaned on the desk and swung his crutch. She wanted to run away, but she would have to walk by both men to leave.

"Larry, what the hell are you talking about?"

"You know damn well what I'm talking about. Jason!"

"Larry, c'mon back to my office." He moved to put his arm around Larry's shoulder, but Larry knocked his arm away. Gregory backed up, and half turned back toward his office. "C'mon, Lar. There's no reason to act like this. We're friends, aren't we?"

"I thought we were." Larry hitched a few feet after him and then stopped. He reached in the canvas bag, feeling for something, keeping his eyes on Gregory.

As Larry withdrew his hand, the few people who had been watching quickly moved behind Alice. The receptionist dived under her desk. The two men who had approached Larry earlier jumped back into the small conference room across the corridor from the receptionist's desk. Gregory froze, arms defensively crossed in front of his chest, mouth open.

"Fuck you!" Larry shouted, as he pulled a sheet of paper from the bag. "I ain't gonna hide in no white collar office, you pile of shit." Then he shouted, "Alice get out here, goddammit."

Alice stepped gingerly out from behind the partition, moving side-step along the wall for a few feet, and then she stopped. Alternately, she moved her hands from her side to cover her mouth and back again. She looked back at the people standing behind her, and wondered if she would ever be able to explain this to them. She took a few more steps and stopped, "It's okay. I need to talk to him."

"Get your ass over here Now!" He screamed like a marine drill sergeant.

"You've been screwing my wife, you no good bastard. Did you all hear that? Your boss has been fucking my wife."

Suddenly everything went silent, as if the great building held its breath. The noise from the street ceased, and even the soft buzz from the fluorescent lights stopped.

Gregory stood motionless. "Larry, what is this? You're drunk."

"Larry, please don't do this," pleaded Alice "You don't know what you're doing. This isn't the way…"

She never finished her sentence. Larry grabbed her by the hair, and threw her to the floor, steadying himself against the wall. She crumpled in a pile in front of the desk, her skirt thrown up to her thighs. She started crying. "I just found out about my son. Except he ain't my son," he sneered. "How's that for news. He's your son."

"Wait a minute," said Gregory. "You think I'm Jason's father?"

"Correction, shit head. I know you're Jason's father."

"Who the hell told you that?"

"How long? How long you been fucking my wife?" yelled Larry.

"You're talking crazy." Gregory looked past Larry toward the two young men in the doorway.

One of them moved from behind. Suddenly Larry whirled around swinging his crutch. He caught the man across the side of his knee. The man grabbed his leg as he fell. He lay on the floor next to the side of the desk as the paper in Larry's hand fluttered to the floor.

"You gonna defend this bastard, you weak shit? Why? You don't know me, and you sure don't know this shithead you work for. He's the father of my two year old son."

Larry looked down at Alice, who had pulled her skirt down to cover her knees. He poked her with his crutch. "Tell 'em, goddammit. Tell 'em."

Gregory started to back down the corridor toward the small conference room.

"What'd she tell you Larry? That we lived together in college? So what. That was years ago."

"Jesus Christ, you think I'm stupid? I thought we were friends, Greg. Why'd you do this to me?" He looked at Alice. "Why'd you do this to me?"

Alice started to get up, but Larry whacked her on the shoulder with his crutch, and fell back against the wall. She balled into a fetal position and covered her head with her arms. Remembering his threats in the hospital room, she knew she was in real trouble.

"I want you to see something, Greg, Look at that," Larry said, pointing to the green-striped NCR computer sheet on the floor. "Go on, read it."

Gregory picked up the paper. He looked at it and then looked at Larry. "What is this," he asked.

"My blood type is A positive," shouted Larry. "Which means I can't have a son with B positive blood."

"Is that what this says? I know how this must look." Gregory took a step toward Larry.

"You think you got it all, don't you. Well, now you got shit."

The elevator pinged. Alice looked up. Larry reached in his bag again, pulling out the Rossi. His hand shook as he aimed it at Gregory's head, less than a foot away. Gregory put his hands in front of his face, palms out.

"Tell them to stay back or he's dead," shouted Larry.

Now people made no pretense about diving for cover. The young man who had thought of tackling Larry tried to scramble under the receptionist's desk with her. The two unarmed security men stopped in the doorway. The squawk of their two-way radios broke the silence.

Larry turned to the hidden audience, and continued. "You want to hear the funny part? I worked my ass off to raise his son. Ain't that a hoot?"

Gregory started backing toward the conference room.

"Don't move, Greg. Don't fucking move. I kill you now, who'd convict me?"

"Larry, don't do this," whimpered Alice. She closed her eyes and put her arms over her head. "You're just upset, but don't go crazy. Put the gun down. Please?"

"You're right. But I'm outta my mind. I'm crazy. I just got out of the hospital and I'm crippled." He paused, and then spoke quietly. "Maybe I should just kill myself."

"Larry, for God's sake. We can work this out. We're friends, me and you. We're fishing buddies, remember?"

"Yeah, me and Jean go fishing, you and Alice hop into bed. I got that picture."

"No, no. That never happened."

"You're a goddam liar." The gun wavered in his hand. He coughed.

The elevator pinged again. Gregory backed up to the wall next to the reception chairs as Larry fired. The slam of the bullet knocked him against the wall, where he slid down to the floor, leaving a red smear on the white cedar wall paneling. His left arm was awkwardly pinned under his body, and his jacket was thrown open. A yelp leaped from several mouths simultaneously. For a second, Larry looked at Gregory, the red stain mushrooming on his white shirt. Then he looked down at Alice and put the barrel of the gun in his mouth.

"My God, Larry, don't."

He fired a second shot which he never heard, splattering the walls and ceiling with pieces of brain matter, bone and blood. At the sound of the second shot, police officers rushed into the room, guns drawn.

The first officer shouted into his shoulder radio. "We got a shooting here, two men down. We need an ambulance right now!" He gave the address and floor, while the second officer went to Gregory who lay unconscious on the floor.

"Looks like this guy'll make it. I won't give odds on his left arm, but I seen worse ones pull through."

The first officer looked at Larry and then went to help Alice. She stumbled to a chair and put her head in her hands, facing the wall.

Tearing open Gregory's shirt, the second officer exposed Gregory's chest, where he saw the bullet hole just below his collarbone and about five inches to the left of his sternum.

Everyone was stunned. Several sat on the floor where they were. The receptionist, who had crawled out from under her desk, was being held by the man who had tried to join her. Alice broke into uncontrollable sobbing as people came out of their safe areas and tried to comfort her. The officers refused to let anyone go until they took statements.

Alice's head was spinning. She felt as if she her strength had been vacuumed out. Less than ten minutes after Larry arrived, the entire episode was over.

The ambulance arrived. Gregory was taken to the hospital. Alice calmed down, her eyes drawn to the body of the man who had once been her husband. He looked peaceful. She walked toward him, her look turning to pity. As she approached, she saw the jagged hole, the missing back of his skull with exposed brain matter and blood still oozing onto the carpet. She looked away, but it was too late. She fell to her hands and knees, and vomited on the carpet next to Larry's canvas bag. Looking through the bag later, she found a photo of Jason and a note scribbled on the back saying "It's all yours." A squad of men arrived, photographed the area, bagged Larry's body, and took it to the morgue.

Alice barely heard the police question people, as if they were speaking from a hilltop far away. There was one piece of information given to the police, about which she heard everyone in the office agree: before Larry shot Gregory and killed himself, he had claimed that Gregory was the father of Alice's son, Jason.

CHAPTER 69

▼

Alice was glad Bill was unaware of the shooting and suicide. Now was the time to confront Gregory. It might not be fitting to see him in the hospital, but there would never be a good time.

She considered what was left of her life and Jason's. She had a house and a mortgage payment. She had to find another job. And she wanted Gregory to admit that Jason was his son.

Why Chicago? Why not California? That's what Maggie said. A new start. Put everything here behind me. Jason could grow up knowing the ocean.

The next morning, as she put on her make-up, the new start and thoughts of Bill became a jumble of swirling images. She sat down on the edge of the bed.

She took the Stevenson, exited at Ohio Street, and headed east to the hospital. The fifty-minute drive gave her time to think. A scene played in her mind. She imagined Jean confronting Gregory, berating him for denying his son and letting some working class mechanic raise him. The thought that they would try to take Jason away faded as she concluded Jean wouldn't want a constant reminder of Gregory's infidelity.

Alice found a metered parking place about a block away and walked to the hospital. She got her visitor's pass, and took the elevator to the fifth floor. The large door to Gregory's hospital room was open, and she walked in, holding the fingers of her left hand with her right in front of her chest.

"Hello, Greg."

CHAPTER 70

▼

Gregory wore hospital pajama bottoms and half a tee shirt, cut to expose a cast from shoulder to wrist. He stood next to his bed and held the headboard with his left hand to steady himself.

He was looking out the window of his small private room, his back to the door. He didn't move when Alice spoke, but continued staring over the roofs of the old two-story stone bungalows that squatted among the high rises between the hospital and the lake.

"I was in surgery for six hours. Six fucking hours. The doctor said I was lucky. The bullet missed the artery."

"I'm sorry, Greg."

"Eventually, I may have full use of my arm." He turned stiffly around. His mouth was distorted into a sneer. "What the hell do you care?" He took a step backwards, and caught his balance on the wall with his left hand. "You've done enough to me. Why don't you get the hell out."

"Greg, I swear, if I had known…" Alice took a step toward him.

"If you had known what? That he wanted to kill me? I came within an inch of being killed. I mean a goddam inch!" He indicated the distance between his thumb and his forefinger.

"Greg, I'm sorry. What can I say. I never imagined that Larry would do anything like that. He doesn't even own a gun. He stole his brother's."

"Well he did it, thanks to you. Look at me. I'm crippled because you were so fucking stupid. I can't believe you actually told him." He walked toward the foot of his bed and grasped the side rail.

"I didn't have a choice. He found out Jason couldn't be his son."

"Give me a break. Did you have to tell him I was the father? Don't you have a fucking brain? Couldn't you have lied? Anything?"

"Don't you think I've asked myself that a thousand times? I had to tell him the truth. I owed him that, at least."

"Bullshit."

"Well, you were the one who fucked me when I was drunk. What did you want me to do? Blame some passing stranger? I didn't tell him you raped me. Maybe he would have aimed lower."

Gregory sat down on the edge of his bed. "I don't know. I thought we had a kind of agreement. I gave you a job. I left you alone. What the hell more did you want. But no. You had to get a case of honesty all of a sudden."

He reached up behind him with his left hand and grabbed the bar suspended over his bed. Groaning, he scooted himself onto the bed and then back to lean against the upraised head of the bed. He stared at the ceiling. Alice sat on the green plastic chair close to the door.

"Seeing you makes me relive the whole terrifying event like it happened ten minutes ago. What do you want me to do? Thank you? Tell you how lucky I am to be alive?"

"I wanted to see how you were doing. I was concerned."

"Well don't be. It's a little late for that. Just get out." He paused a moment. "And clean out your desk, too."

"It's done. I still can't believe that it happened."

"You can't?" he said, his eyes widening. "Look at me. I know it happened. You can't imagine the terror of looking at a gun in the hand of a crazy drunk."

"What do you want me to say? I told you I didn't know."

"Every time I take my shirt off for the rest of my life, I'll remember. Do you realize they had to take out my shoulder blade? It was shattered. In addition to the scars, I'll have the stiffness as a permanent reminder."

"Really? A permanent reminder. You mean like a child that I wash and dress every day? I have my reminders. Do you know our daughter would have been seven this year." Tears slid down her cheeks.

"That's a choice you made. I had nothing to do with that."

"You asshole. You had everything to do with it. Why the hell do you think I made that choice?"

Gregory continued to stare at the ceiling.

"Jean's divorcing you isn't she?"

"You got that right. She informed me last night that she wants to take over the agency."

"Take over the agency? Can she? You don't own it."

"I told her she could have the house, the Cadillac, but he said she'd probably get 'em anyway. No, she wants to be a managing partner. She'd sit right there, along with my father and me. And Schwartz. They'll be overjoyed, I'm sure."

"Well, you are married. Jean has every right to half of what you own."

"And there's no way I can stop her," he continued, as if she had said nothing. "If I fight her, I create a scandal that could bankrupt the agency, and everybody loses. If I don't fight her, I get to see her at every board meeting."

Alice smiled a begrudging admiration for Jean.

I wish I had done as much. All I got was equity in the house, along with a mortgage. "All this is your fault, dammit. How could you have been so goddam dumb? All you had to do was keep your mouth shut, and everything would've been fine. Oh, shit." he closed his eyes and winced in pain. Tears trickled down his cheeks. "All you had to do was keep your fucking mouth shut."

Alice walked to the window and sat on the deep ledge. "There's another reason I came here. It's Jason. This may be a bad time, but he is your son."

"Don't even go there."

She realized she didn't despise him anymore. He was pathetic.

Was there ever a time when we wanted to change the world? When people were important? Or has he always been this way, and I was too blind to comprehend.

"If you want money from me," he continued, "you'll have to prove that Jason's my son. In court."

"Is that what you want? A paternity suit? A court fight, complete with DNA testing?"

"What've I got to lose? Now, it's your word against mine."

"No. It's your word against Jason's. He's the only one who'll lose out in all this."

She couldn't treat Jason as if he were a paste-board character. If it came to a court case, she would do without Gregory's help.

"If you don't accept him now, you may never have another chance. I covered for you for almost three years, and that was my mistake. I won't make it again. I think it would be a good idea for you to see Jason when you get out. I told him what happened, even though he doesn't really understand."

"You told him? Is there anyone you didn't tell? Maybe we ought to get the six o'clock news in on this."

Gregory slid down in bed and rolled on his side. Alice left without looking back.

CHAPTER 71

▼

Hiking alone in the late afternoon at Kettle Moraine State Park, Bill again considered the pros and cons of telling Alice everything. She knew he had been in a war where whole villages were reduced to smoldering charcoal. They saw it all on the ten o'clock news and looked the other way, preferring blissful ignorance.

What's to be gained by telling her? Fear. What's to be gained by not telling her? Safety.

When Bill returned from his hike to the old fire tower, he saw a message at the ranger station. He found the public phone and dialed Alice's number.

CHAPTER 72

▼

"Alice, what's happened? I just picked up the message at the ranger station."

"Oh, Bill, Jason's disappeared. I can't find him anywhere. I called my parents, but they're no help in an emergency. I didn't know who else to call."

"Have you called the police?"

"Yes, and they've already gone door to door. They said there was nothing they could do until tomorrow."

"Call Larry. He ought to be there to help out." Alice became silent. Bill wondered if the line had been disconnected. Then he heard her muffled sobs.

"There's been a terrible accident. Larry's dead."

Bill was unable to speak for a moment. "Oh, my God. I'll be there as fast as I can. It's almost 5:30. I should be there by 9:30, 10 at the latest. Everything'll be okay. Go and talk to the neighbors again. Maybe someone'll remember something."

Alice walked outside. The light blue sky, spotted with cottony clouds, had hints of darker colors to the west. She went to Mrs. Garvey's house.

"Now, don't you worry, Alice. Kids have a way of wandering off and coming back. My oldest boy ran off once and didn't come back for two days. He'll get hungry and you'll see him."

Alice felt drained. "He's only two. Where could he go?" It was as if all her blood had been sucked from her body and her bones had been removed, leaving helpless tentacles.

"Here's a pillow. Put your head down for a few minutes."

Alice closed her eyes and stretched out on the sofa. "You'd think the police would be able to do something. It's like they gave up. They talked to a few people and then quit."

When she opened her eyes, she was alone in the room and Mrs. Garvey was in the kitchen. Mrs. Garvey walked through the door carrying two cups.

"I made us some tea."

"How long have I been out?" she asked.

"Only a few minutes." She paused. "I heard the news about Larry. I'm so sorry. I know that doesn't help."

"Thanks, Mrs. Garvey. I appreciate your kindness. I think the whole thing is like something out of Kafka. I can't believe this is happening to me."

"Why don't you stay here tonight. I made some soup and chicken, and there's more than I can eat."

"Thanks, but I can't. Someone might call about Jason, and I've got to be home. Bill's on his way back from Wisconsin."

Alice took a few sips of her tea, excused herself, and then walked across the lawn to her own house. The coming night was clearly visible in the distance. The huge orange ball was making an unsuccessful attempt to beat back the darkness. Another time, the sunset would have been beautiful.

Alice moved the portable phone to the small table next to the sofa and lay down with her head next to it. The phone would wake her if she fell asleep.

CHAPTER 73

▼

It was dark when Bill pulled up. The door was unlocked, and he put the lights on as he entered. Alice jumped up from the sofa, ran to him, and threw her arms around his neck, clinging like a frightened cat. "Oh, God, I'm frantic," she whined into his shoulder, her voice shrill and breathy. "We've scouted the neighborhood, and there's no sign of him anywhere. I haven't seen him since this morning at breakfast."

"And the police didn't turn up anything?"

"Nothing. They told me they'd send someone out again tomorrow. I gave them his picture."

"Does he know about Larry?"

"Yes. I also told him that Gregory's really his father."

"God. That's a hell of a lot for a two year old to assimilate. Did he seem upset?"

"Of course he's upset. He doesn't understand what's happening. I'm not sure I do. I'm sorry. I guess I'm taking out my frustration on you."

"Driving back gave me a lot of time to think. You don't think Gregory or Jean would do something? Do you?"

"What do you mean?"

"You know, have someone take him?"

"Kidnap? That's what the police asked. Gregory told me he'd never have anything to do with Jason. Told me I'd have to go to court if I wanted anything from him."

"Anything's possible. But you're probably right. Maybe Jason's hiding somewhere."

"I don't know. The police looked everywhere. The thought of my little boy hiding somewhere. It's dark." Her voice started to quiver. "Damn, this's no time to fall apart. We've got to do something."

"I know. But what?"

She sat next to Bill on the sofa. He put his arm around her shoulder, and pulled her to him. Putting her head on his chest, her tears made dark blue spots on his denim shirt.

"I remember when I ran away," he said, stroking her hair. I was older than Jason, about a month after my seventh birthday." Bill spoke slowly, in a hoarse whisper. "I was younger than Andrew was when he died."

Alice looked up at him and found him staring out the window into the night as he spoke. She could feel his body tense, as if he were ready for a fight.

"I don't see what this had to do with anything. Jason is missing. I'm so upset my head is pounding, and you tell me stories about your childhood."

"I don't know why I'm telling you now. Maybe I'm trying to understand how Jason feels."

"So, why did you run away?"

"I was angry for being deceived when I found out my father had changed his name. I thought he didn't trust me. He told me I was too young to understand things. He told me when he applied for a job, someone named George Forrest got the interview, and Isaac Baumgarten was told there were no openings. I asked him about family. He said, 'There is no family,' and he never talked about it again."

"You never told me."

"I don't think I've ever told anyone. I was so upset I never wanted to see them again. I didn't want to be the son of parents who were so deceitful. But I didn't know where to go, so I stole a salami from the pantry and hid under the porch. I hid there for a long time. I remember it was dark when my father finally carried me into the house." Tears were wetting Bill's cheeks when he finished.

"What about your mother? What'd she do? She must've been frantic."

"I think they knew where I was. It was their way..." he stopped and pushed Alice from him, holding her shoulders. "Is there any way to crawl under the front porch?"

"No. It's built on a slab. But there's a low crawl space under the room addition. And there's an access panel in the basement behind the refrigerator. Why didn't the police look there?"

"They didn't know there was one."

"But who could squeeze in there behind the refrigerator?"

"A two-year old."

In the basement, Bill wedged his body between the refrigerator and the wall and pushed, moving the refrigerator. The small access door was slightly open. It squealed noisily as he forced it open enough to wedge his bulk through. He crawled in a short way. He could see nothing in the blackness. He called back to Alice to bring him a flashlight. The dampness slid over his head and arms, making him shiver. The crawl space was a square tunnel, about three feet wide and two feet high, with a dirt floor and the concrete walls running the length of the room above. Long nails stuck down from the flooring above like irregular teeth in a monstrous mouth. At the end was what seemed to be a small opening in the left wall. He would need to crawl the entire length of the room addition in the dirt on his knees and elbows to reach it. He sneezed several times. As he inched along, the light wavered eerily in his hand, bouncing off the walls and the dirt floor. Silvery trails left by slugs were disturbed ahead of him, so he knew Jason was down here somewhere. The damp earth smelled of mildew and rotten wood, and his teeth ground and snapped with the grit in his mouth. After he had crept the length of the first section and scooted through the opening, he stopped and listened, turning off the light. The darkness engulfed him, but he could see a small light at the end of the second section, only a few feet from where he had started, had he been able to move through the concrete wall. It was a small screened opening in the floor above him, to allow moisture to escape. Listening in the darkness, he heard a faint scratching noise, and called out to Jason. Alice heard the shout. No reply. He was afraid the scratching could be mice or rats. He heard the sound again. It was too regular to be a rat. He aimed the light to the end, and saw Jason's head peering at him from the end of the section. He crawled toward him. The scratching had been Jason, marking with a stone on the concrete wall in the dim light of the screened opening. He sat cross-legged in the dirt, his face dirty where dust had stuck to wiped tears.

"He's here, just below the grate in the floor." Bill crawled the rest of the way to Jason.

"Jason, why didn't you answer me?" Jason shrugged his shoulders. "Your mother's really worried that something awful'd happened to you."

They could hear Alice's feet clacking along the floor above them toward the grate.

"No, she isn't. She's happy I'm gone. Now I can't make any more trouble for her." Above, Alice cried silently and hugged her knees, rocking slowly back and forth on the bathroom floor.

"What trouble? You never made trouble for her," said Bill.

Jason started to cry. "Then how come daddy's gone away and Uncle Greg's in the hospital?"

Bill took Jason on his lap, he hugged him.

"And mommy said that Uncle Greg's really my daddy," Jason sniffled into Bill's chest. "I thought daddy was my daddy." He wiped tears, mucous, and dirt on Bill's shirt.

"Oh, Jason, I'm so sorry," Alice's plaintive cry cut through the grate. "Can you hear me? I love you. Please. Come back up here." She ran back to the basement.

Jason looked up at Bill, his face shadowed in the faint light from above.

"It's okay, Jason," said Bill. "Let's go back. Here, you take the flashlight and I'll crawl behind you."

Jason shined the light ahead and started crawling with Bill right behind him. His feet kicked up some dirt that made Bill sneeze again. As they rounded the first opening, they could see the light from the doorway streaming toward them, like a beacon. When Jason squeezed through the doorway, Alice pulled him to her, squeezing him in a bear hug.

Jason started crying, "I'm sorry, mommy," he sobbed, the words coming out in bursts through short breaths, between sobs.

"Shhh," she said, gently rocking him and crying. She started laughing.

Bill eased through the opening and dusted himself off. "Nothing like a little scramble in a crawl space to end the evening," he smiled. He slid the small door closed and pushed the refrigerator back in place.

Alice put Jason down and squatted in front of him. Dried clumps of mud were matted in his hair and smeared over his face. Several swipes of grime crossed his shirt where he'd wiped his hands. One blob of muck balanced on the end of his shoe, and another was caught between his shoe and his sock.

"You must be starved," Alice finally said to her son. "What would you like for dinner? After showers, of course."

"McDonald's" shouted Jason, before the echo of her words faded in the air.

"Well, let's clean up and get going."

CHAPTER 74

▼

Alice was on the wrack of her dilemma: pursue the budding relationship with Bill or start a new life. California made her heart race for the freshness of the undiscovered.

If I stay, I'll have to face people who know the sordid story of my relationship with Larry and Gregory. If I leave, no one in California would have heard of it.

It was at the Lake Bluff Labor Day picnic that Alice told Bill about her decision. The day was bright but overcast, a cool fall day that hints of fall and winter with muted shadows. Sarah and George were there. Watching and running after Jason didn't give Alice much time to talk to Bill. They were sitting on a bench near the playground.

"Jason and I really need a change, Bill. I've decided to accept Maggie's invitation and go out to California."

"I sort of expected you would."

"I don't know if it'll be just a long visit or for good. I put the house on the market."

"You sure it's a good time?"

"I've got no job, and very little chance of getting one here. Gregory refuses to answer any of my calls. I heard from someone in the office—one of the few who will talk to me—that he's doing most of his work outside the Chicago area. He's got an apartment in New York and won't even come to meetings when Jean's there. The problem is she's good. She's already brought in two new accounts. Nishan and Abe Schwartz don't seem to have any problems with her work."

"What about work? You going to be able to get a job there?"

"Maggie's lined up an interview with Frankel. She even started looking for an apartment for the three of us in the Redondo Beach area. She says we can't afford a place on the Strand, but there're nice places just off Pacific Coast Highway in Hermosa or Manhattan Beach."

The drive back was in silence. Jason slept, and neither Bill nor Alice had anything to say.

CHAPTER 75

▼

Bill pulled up in the driveway. It was early Wednesday morning. His first class was not until one in the afternoon. September was well on its way. Teaching at the college gave him a sense of completeness in his life. He hadn't been contacted by the police for several months. Probably the lack of manpower he'd read about placed the Morse case low on their priority.

But his happiness at work clashed with his personal life. He wanted events to mesh, like interlocking gears. He suspected they never would. Endings and death chattered in the gear-box, always threatening to grind to a halt, like Morse's life.

He sat in his Pathfinder for a few minutes staring at the "FOR SALE" sign in the front yard of Alice's house. It reminded him of a gallows, hanging loosely from the cross beam, swinging back and forth as the slight breeze alternately blew and stopped. The morning clouds signaled a coming darkness.

He wanted to ask Morse about the crushing darkness. Is there ever brightness on the other side? He eased himself from the driver's seat.

Alice saw him and opened the door. She hated moments when people become clumsy. Catching the heel of her shoe on the threshold, she almost stumbled, steadying herself with her hand on the large brass door handle. She fought a sudden urge to run to him, throw her arms around his neck and shout, "I changed my mind. I'm staying!" Instead, she looked at his shoes, like a child about to hear something she didn't like.

"So you're really going to California. Can't say I blame you. I'd probably do the same thing if I were you." *Stupid thing to say.* He tried to convince himself that her leaving was the best for him as well, but his thoughts crunched underfoot like dry wood shavings.

He had wanted to be honest, to tell Alice the truth. He also felt this abrupt break was better than a slow, painful dance of disappearance. This was an ending that could be blamed on circumstance.

"I can sell the house for almost twice what I thought I could," she said hesitantly, as if expecting his approval. "Maggie's got room for Jason and me to stay with her until we find something. You know how she loves Jason. She's his only aunt." Alice stopped, but the silence startled her. "You could always come out there for a visit.

Bill wanted to turn and run. "Sure. Yeah. I sure could do that. Visit, I mean."

"Wanna come in for a cup of coffee? I've still got a lot of packing for the movers, but I could use the break."

"Sure, that'd be nice. Easier to talk in the house than out here in the street. "You need any help?" He wanted to retract the words. He wanted to say good-bye and leave.

Alice had been holding the handle of the door, as if she were afraid to let go, blocking his entrance. She opened it wider and allowed him to enter ahead of her. "No, I think I can manage. Thanks, anyway."

He walked directly to the kitchen and sat down at the table, leaning against the wall as he had done many times. He watched her as she entered the room, reflecting on the times she had made coffee after they had come home from the movies or had made love. He would miss those evenings, the warmth of her arms, the honesty of her smile.

Alice made coffee but didn't sit down. She stood at the sink, her back to him. She watched the coffee filling up the pot, listened to the hiss as some water hit the plate, smelled the aroma of hazelnut. As she filled two cups, she knew she would have to say something. She brought the cups to the table.

"Want a piece of cake or some cookies?"

"No, thanks. This's fine."

Why do people's faces change after you get to know them?

She tried to imagine she was looking at him for the first time, but intimacy distorted her view. She now saw lines around his mouth and eyes. There were two deep grooves from above his nostrils to the corners of his mouth She tried to conjure up that first image. She couldn't do it.

They started speaking simultaneously, and then both stopped.

"Go ahead," he half mumbled. "You first."

"This's hard, Bill. You're not making it very easy."

"I know. I don't know how to make it easy."

She took a sip of coffee and then continued. "Sure you don't want anything?"

He shook his head. "Naw. I'm not going to stay long. I don't know what to say. You need to get away from here, and I can't. It's that simple. Better to make a fresh start."

"You can't have a fresh start without letting go of the past. And the only way to let go is to take it out and throw it away, like garbage. Too bad we couldn't make the fresh start together. At the same time."

"Yeah."

She wanted him to tell her what rooted him to his dark spot. She had learned that only by releasing could anyone move on in life, and that holding back was a road-block. It stopped everything. She could tell him, but it was not a lesson that could be taught. It was one that must be learned the way she did it—the hard way.

He felt her pressure to do the one thing he refused. Tell the truth. Until Marissa died, he had always believed that things work out for the best, that somehow, somewhere there might just be a god who looked down at his toy people, happy he has them, making up stories for them to act out. After, there had been darkness. God had been called for dinner, and had kicked his toy people under the bed.

"Y'know, maybe it's for the best. This way, there's no anger."

Alice reached across and touched the back of his hand as he held the cup.

"I know." It not the swallowed-up kind of hurt she felt when Gregory left her, that made things dark and angry. Not the crushing kind she felt married to Larry, that make her hold her breath and fear the next moment. This was like the tooth-ache that throbs beneath the surface.

Bill sipped the last of his coffee and stared into the cup. He wondered why he felt as bad as he did. He had become aware that since the shooting, Alice had changed. She had become relaxed, even happier. He had no idea why. "So, when're you actually leaving?"

"Tomorrow. I never learned to leave early enough to avoid traffic. Bill, I'm sorry. About everything. Sorry I dragged you into the whole mess. But I'm glad you were there. I don't know what I'd've done without your support,"

"You're stronger than you give yourself credit for. You're starting over. From nothing."

Alice knew she loved Bill as much as she had ever loved anyone. But he was a windowless tower with one door that could free him, and it was closed. She wanted him to ask her to stay. But she knew that if he did, she'd hate it.

The phone rang. It was her mother, reminding Alice that she had promised to bring Jason for lunch.

Bill looked at his watch. "I guess I better get going."

Alice hugged him, warming in his bear-like grasp, and then walked him out to his SUV. She wondered if she should tell him she loved him, but decided to say nothing. What would be the point. Then she kissed him lightly on the cheek and went in to get Jason.

He started his Pathfinder. Looking at his watch, he would just have time for lunch in the faculty cafeteria before his afternoon class.

0-595-27527-3

Printed in the United States
23210LVS00006B/133-159